BOOK 3 IN THE CERBERUS SERIES

ISBN: 978-1-955622-56-1

Published by

Fideli Publishing, Inc.
119 W. Morgan St.
Martinsville, IN 46151

www.FideliPublishing.com

SOLARA

Characters

Dan Ronin, Capt. – Captain of *Cerberus*

Diane Mueller, Cmdr. – Commanding Officer (XO) of *Cerberus*

Elvis Lazarus, Lt. Cmdr. – Chief Engineer, *Cerberus*

Pierre Delacroix, Lt. – Sensors, *Cerberus*

Kristoff Alphonso, Lt. – Fabrication, *Cerberus*

Matt LeCroy, Lt. – Tactical, *Cerberus*

Marcy Anzio, Lt. – Weapons, *Cerberus*

Maria Delgado, Lt. – Communications, *Cerberus*

Hirohito Taketa, Lt., Chief Medical Officer – Medical, *Cerberus*

Chrizanne "Anne" Abara, Nurse – Medical, *Cerberus*

Antonio Perez, Lt. – Helm, *Cerberus*

Kelvin Sunderland, Lt. – Commander Air Group (CAG), *Cerberus*

Erin Johnson, Pilot Officer – Bulldog 1 pilot

Hal Patterson, Chief – Bulldog 1 rearseater

Antonio Russo, Pilot Officer – Bulldog 3 pilot

Michael Jonsey, Chief – Bulldog 3 rearseater

Greg Lowridge – Bulldog 7 Pilot Officer

Paul Drayson – Bulldog 7 rearseater

Adolph Gustav– Marine Lieutenant

Brett Mackey – Marine Bravo team

Ed Wilson – Marine Bravo team

Terry Allison – Marine Bravo team

Ty Jeffries – Marine Bravo team

Toshi Kanagawa – Marine Echo team

Adrian "The Pirate" Longman – Marine Echo team

Julio Gonzales – Marine Echo team

Hiro "Gung Ho" Gozen – Marine Echo Team

Victor Berger – Marine Gamma team

David "Olé" Addington – Marine Gamma team

Juan Diaz – Marine Gamma team

Aldo Pena – Marine Gamma team

Prisha Gadre, Ambassador – Protocol Officer, Terra Station

Dr. Winston Wright – Protocol Officer, *Cerberus*

Leroy Greene – Junior Protocol Officer, *Cerberus*

Jessup Rodding, Admiral –Wayside Station

Hobson, Colonel– Fleet Intelligence

Frida Enginnsdottir – Ullrian Shieldmaiden

Jørgen Freyr – Ullrian warlord

Seth Galruud – Ullrian Sojourner

Leif Galruud – Ullrian Chieftain

Lars Berven –Ullrian Captain of *Warspite*

Ivar Haraldson –Ullrian Warrior

Eric the Dour – Ullrian Warrior

Anders Halfhand – Ullrian Captain of *Storm Bringer*

Don Tony Morelino – Head of the Morelino family, Cosa Nostra

Duke Lordano, Morelino family consigliere, Cosa Nostra

Franco (Frankie) Ricci – President of the Leadership Council on Il Mio Dieci, Cosa Nostra

Luca Bianci – Heavy equipment manager on Il Mio Dieci, Cosa Nostra

Joey Saldano – Captain, Cosa Nostra Raider No. 16

Tommy Votto –Tactical Officer, Cosa Nostra Raider No. 16

Jeanie Crespi –Comms Officer, Cosa Nostra Raider No. 16

Eddie Vega –Pilot, Cosa Nostra Raider No. 16

CHAPTER 1

WAYSIDE STATION

s Cerberus slowly entered the Wayside Station docking area, Adm. Jessup Rodding and Colonel Hobson shared a quick glance. Their looks expressed a lot, although neither made a sound. The two were standing in an area that gave them a view of Cerberus from below the ship's port side. An ugly, blackened scar marred the ship's hull and looked even darker than the hull's matte-black, diamond-composite coating.

After a few minutes, Hobson cleared his throat. "My people are itching to study the tech behind the beams that damaged Cerberus at such a distance." As he spoke, Hobson never took his eyes from Cerberus.

Rodding, hands clasped behind his back, nodded thoughtfully. "We got lucky. Cerberus could have been destroyed, and we would have written them off when we never heard from them again. Who knows how long it would have been before we would have tried to travel to the system where Terra Station is located. Might have been centuries."

"Are you going to send Cerberus out to Terra Station again? Getting into a shooting war with a lost colony is pretty controversial," Hobson asked, turning his head away slightly to face Rodding.

Rodding shook his head. "No. We have other ships that can handle missions to Terra Station. We need Cerberus for exploration because we have so few with her capabilities, and that includes the experience of her officers and crew. She was only away for about three months when she was supposed to be gone for at least a year. We'll patch her back up, restock the shelves and replace needed personnel."

Hobson shook his head in disbelief. "Hard to wrap my head around what Cerberus managed to accomplish in such a short period of time. Winning the war on Earth. Interstellar exploration. Discovering an unknown lost colony. Fighting and winning a war on said colony. Returning home with battle damage still showing. Just incredible."

Rodding smiled a humorless half-smile at Hobson's summation of Cerberus' activities over the past year or so. "Knowing how horrified Captain Ronin and Commander Muller were by the fame they achieved when the war on Earth was won, they won't be able to go back to deep space fast enough. Did you know I tried to promote Commander Muller twice already?"

That was news to Hobson. "No, I didn't. I wondered why she wasn't captaining her own command already."

"She's certainly earned it. But the only available commands involve ships that stay in this solar system, so Commander Mueller deems the prudent course of action is to stay on Cerberus and escape the curse of fame by returning to deep space. And, like Captain Ronin, she has the itch to go forth and explore. Cerberus is currently the only game in town to do both," Rodding said, as he watched Cerberus come to a stop and begin docking with Wayside.

"Maybe she'll change her mind now that they've returned?" Hobson asked.

Rodding snorted. "That WAS her latest response. She just sent it a few hours ago."

Hobson's eyebrows shot up. Wearing a thoughtful expression on his face, he turned again to look at Rodding. "Mueller's not wrong. At this point, the prime crew of Cerberus is so famous that naval rank promotions really don't mean much, unless it's to a posting that takes them far enough away they can live their lives in peace."

"Agreed. The prime crew seems to have conspired to stay together and get out of the solar system as much as they can," Rodding said. "The Admiralty has considered promoting Captain Ronin over his objections and breaking the crew up to distribute their experience among other postings, but those considerations keep getting overridden. They finally decided Cerberus' missions are so perilous that the best strategy for mission success is to keep the ship's prime crew intact. We'll tell them that at today's debriefing."

Now Hobson snorted softly. "They'll either be glad to hear that, or take after us with torches and pitchforks."

CHAPTER 2

DEBRIEFING

"**C**aptain, Commander, the Admiral is ready to see you now," said Rodding's orderly. She opened the wooden doors leading to the Admiral's inner sanctum and motioned for them to proceed inside.

Ronin and Mueller, wearing their gray shipboard uniforms, stood and quickly walked into Rodding's office. They came to attention and saluted when they saw Rodding and Hobson.

"At ease, you two. Grab a seat and we'll get started. Colonel, you want to do the honors?" Rodding said as he motioned for them to occupy the chairs arranged around his desk.

"With pleasure, Admiral," Hobson said as he stood and stepped over to the Admiral's cabinet. He opened it up to reveal an expensive-looking bottle of dark caramel-colored Old Prohibition bourbon and four glasses. Hobson looked back at the others and asked, "On the rocks, or neat?"

A chorus of "neat" came almost simultaneously, causing Hobson to laugh softly to himself. Over the past few years of meetings in Rodding's office, they had all followed the Admiral's lead and become purists who didn't sully the fine bourbon with barbaric additives like ice cubes.

As Hobson poured a few fingers of the bourbon into each highball glass, Rodding leaned forward and took a good look at his officers. "First things first. The Admiralty has decided to honor your wishes and keep you at your current ranks and posting. Sometime in the future you might be promoted against your wishes, but that's a problem for another time."

Ronin and Mueller smiled tired smiles. The trip home was short enough that they still hadn't caught up on the sleep they missed during the Terra Station War. "Thank you, Admiral. That's pretty good news from our perspective," Ronin replied.

"I have better news for you. You'll get two weeks of leave to restock your ship's cupboards and have the shipyard finish the repairs before you return to deep space," Rodding said as Hobson handed out the glasses of Old Prohibition. The four clinked their glasses and murmured cheers, before taking slow, appreciative sips of the fine bourbon.

"We're going to need some more Marines, sir," Mueller noted as she set down her glass.

Rodding's face broke into a lopsided grin. "Commander, we put out the word for volunteers before you got the ship home. The sheer number of Marines trying to sign on for your next trip into the dark will keep Lieutenant Adolph Gustav busy for days just trying to sort through them all." Rodding paused to take a sip.

Ronin asked the question at the top of his and Mueller's minds. "Are we returning to Terra Station, Admiral?"

Shaking his head, Rodding replied, "No, we have other ships that can handle that mission. You're mostly returning to the original parameters of your last mission. Go and search for the Lost Colonies. It hadn't occurred to the Admiralty before you stumbled across Terra Station that there might also be uncharted colonies in addition to the Lost Colonies of Solara, Forrestal and Celestra. So, now your mission parameters have been updated to include uncharted colonies as well."

Hobson, now sitting in one of the chairs, spoke up. "We've already set the boffins in the station's research labs to work on a problem you encountered during the trip to Terra Station. Once you were engaged by that planet's military regime, Cerberus faced the choice of leaving the civilians unguarded and returning to Earth, or protecting them by eliminating the threat. While the Admiralty strongly believes Cerberus took the proper course of action given those two extremes, having another option available to choose from would be to your benefit."

Hobson took a quick sip of the Old Prohibition before continuing. The pause allowed him to build the suspense; he was not without a sense of dramatic flair.

"The boffins are working on building a long-range message drone with a jump drive that meets the criteria you outlined in your report. If the ship needs to call in help or reinforcements, or whatever, such a drone can be sent home," Hobson concluded.

Ronin and Mueller shared a quick glance. Ronin had reported something similar in his logs that had been sent ahead, but he was somewhat surprised they had been reviewed and acted upon so quickly.

Nodding, Ronin quickly said, "That would be an exceptionally good idea, Colonel. When we're that far away from this solar system, a lifeline back to Earth can become critically important. We just hadn't appreciated quite how important before embarking on the trip to Terra Station."

Rodding finished his drink and cast a measuring look at his officers. "OK. Dan, get the rest of your team's recommendations to my office by late second shift, local station time. We'll regroup on an ad hoc basis for the next couple weeks to prepare Cerberus for departure. We'll have a more thorough debriefing by week's end, but for now, you two are dismissed. Oh, and you both might want to stay in the military areas of the station for now."

Mueller and Ronin shared an alarmed glance. "Trouble, sir?" Mueller asked for them both.

"Only if you consider an unbearable interest by the media in your presence here an issue. We can keep them away from you in the military controlled areas," Rodding said with a sardonic grin.

"Sir, isn't the Battle of Earth old news by now? I should think they'd start to lose interest by now," Ronin said with a frustrated look on his face.

Hobson half-smiled as he shook his head slightly. "'Fraid not, Captain. And once they hear of this little soirée over Terra Station, you'll simply be chum for the sharks."

Ronin's eyes closed slightly as he unwittingly sighed and rested his forehead in his left hand. He wasn't aware that Mueller unintentionally mimicked him. They both were dealing with feelings of revulsion at being the object of so much media obsession.

"No such luck. If you want my advice, you'd be better off getting Cerberus back into deep space and leaving us all behind," Rodding said with a knowing expression on his face. He knew these two pretty well by now.

Ronin and Mueller looked at each other again. Their expressions were nearly identical. The same old dread. Like a couple of people who just wanted to be left alone, but the hounding of the media left no place for them to hide. By now, Rodding and Hobson knew that look well.

"Yessir," Ronin said, drawling the two words together like many of the members of his crew tended to do. "We'll get the ship ready for the next flight operations and depart as soon as we can."

***

A few hours later, Ronin stopped by to see Lieutenant Gustav down in the Marine Country section of Cerberus. Gustav looked both tired and frustrated as he sat in his tiny office. He had been interviewing potential replacement candidates ever since Ronin passed the word to the crew to get the ship ready to depart.

Ronin stopped short of the threshold to Gustav's door and listened.

"Lance Corporal Gozen, tell me why you want to join Echo team?" Although it was phrased as a question, at this point the nearly exhausted Gustav basically said it as an order.

Lance Cpl. Hiro Gozen didn't even make an attempt at toning down his enthusiasm. "Sir, Echo team, and all the Cerberus Marine teams, have encountered and overcome some of the most challenging missions in the entire Corps! Its leadership has been both exemplary and highly skilled in the face of particularly difficult and notably unique circumstances. Sir, isn't benefiting from good leadership and our training to adapt and overcome part of the whole reason why we joined the Corps in the first place?" Gozen's answer was not only overly enthusiastic; it was smart and perceptive.

Gustav was impressed despite his exhaustion. "Yes, it is, Lance Corporal. And I've discovered that crazy adventures, exploring strange new cultures and the chance to engage interesting people in interstellar firefights also seems to have piqued the interest of much of the Corps for recruitment purposes."

Gozen suddenly grinned. It was a winning smile. "Oh, yessir! Those things, too. But it's more than just that for me. Everyone wants to join a winning enterprise, and serving aboard Cerberus is the top of the food pyramid in terms of winning. Especially when you've experienced the opposite side of the coin. It lends a whole different perspective to why I'm want to serve with the best now. Better chances of survival and success, and the opportunity to learn from the best. A Marine can't ask for much more than that."

Gustav nodded thoughtfully at Gozen's somewhat vague reference to what can happen to a team that is poorly led. He knew Gozen was thinking of the Teller Incident, which occurred several years ago during the war. The vainglorious Teller was a Marine lieutenant who had confused his inflated sense of self-importance with actual leadership ability. Teller was the type of leader who was always blaming his men or others for his own failures. He wasn't smart enough to listen to the valuable combat experience of his team sergeants, and he always took credit for the achievements of his men. The lieutenant's flaws resulted in a poorly led team with rock-bottom morale.

Teller's service to the Corps ended with what became known as the Teller Incident. Teller had intentionally disregarded the orders of his superiors by racing ahead of the other units in a misguided attempt to reach and secure a heavily defended objective. His team was slaughtered. Only the leadership of the surviving team sergeant enabled a small handful of Marines, including Gozen, to survive. Teller did not live to learn from his mistakes, nor did many of the Marines under his leadership live to learn from Teller's mistakes.

"I agree, Lance Corporal. Echo team is a well-led, on-the-bounce team of highly motivated and close-knit Marines. They've been through a lot, but they are spirited and walk like champions with their heads held high and a steely glint in their glares. I get the feeling you can be a successful part of that kind of team.

"Echo 1 is Gunnery Sgt. Toshi Kanagawa. He's a natural leader, and very experienced in combat. I'm letting him know I'm sending you on to him for your next interview, and we'll get back to you and the other candidates after we've had time to talk things over. Cerberus is on a tight schedule, so we won't keep you waiting long."

"Thank you sir! I won't let the team down!" Gozen stood and saluted. Gustav returned the salute and shook hands. Gozen left, saluting Ronin as he encountered him outside the office.

"Sorry, Captain! I didn't realize you were there," Gozen said.

"At ease, Lance Corporal. I need to borrow the Lieutenant now that you're done with him, so I won't hold you up," Ronin said, smiling as he dismissed Gozen.

"Captain, what brings you down to the nether regions of Marine Country?" Gustav asked as he poked his head outside his office to confirm it actually was Ronin outside the door.

"Is it just me, or do the Marine ranks seem to be getting younger?" Ronin asked in response.

Gustav snorted. "They're definitely getting younger, sir. Some of the privates who came in for interviews were so new, they were still wet from birth."

Ronin chuckled. It was a running joke among the aging warhorses in the fleet like themselves. "How goes the interviewing? Finding qualified candidates?" he asked as they both took a seat in the cramped little office.

"Yessir. The good news is just about every Marine aboard Wayside Station is trying to get a billet aboard Cerberus, so we have plenty to pick from. The bad news is just about every Marine aboard Wayside Station is trying to get a billet aboard Cerberus, so we have to spend a lot of time picking from them," said Gustav, succinctly summarizing the problem.

"Other than Chief Lazarus and repairs to the ship, you drew the shortest straw on getting Cerberus turned around and back into the dark. I don't want to take up your time unnecessarily, but I was nearby and just wanted to tell you if there's anything you need from the rest of us, just ask and I'll do my best to make it happen."

Ronin stood, and so did Gustav as he replied, "Thank you Captain! You'll hear of any problems first, then. I'm collecting candidates like Gozen while we're here, and if there's more like him out there, we'll be in good shape."

Ronin nodded. "Sounds good. I'll get out of your hair then and have some coffee sent in. Looks like we both could use some," he said before turning to leave.

"Off to see the good *Dr.* Wright, then?" Gustav said, raising an eyebrow and emphasizing the word "doctor." It didn't take a genius to figure out why Ronin was headed for caffeinated reinforcement.

Ronin stopped, turning slightly and sighing. "They just can't make coffee strong enough sometimes," he replied with a tired grin, before leaving.

Gustav nodded to himself. "Coffee, goooood," he growled in his best caveman like voice. *Can never have too much coffee*, he thought, as he keyed up the next applicant's file on his screen.

CHAPTER 3

THE DARK

"**W**ayside Station Control has cleared Cerberus for departure, Captain, and all ship departments report manned and ready. *Dr.* Wright would like you to know that the protocol officers are also ready," Lieutenant Delgado reported from her communications station, turning to face Ronin, who was seated in the command chair. To Delgado's credit, she kept a straight face as she stated the bit about the protocol officers and subtly emphasizing Wright's title.

Ronin closed his eyes slightly and pinched the bridge of his nose like he was trying to ward off a migraine headache. He then looked up and at the helm. "Lieutenant Perez, disengage docking clamps and make ready for departure."

Perez nodded in return, and replied, "Aye, aye. Docking clamps disengaged. Engaging primary thrusters. Ready to depart."

"Take us out, Mr. Perez," Ronin ordered.

"Aye, Captain. Taking Cerberus out," Perez noted, sounding somewhat distracted because he was busy entering the commands to make the ship move.

Ronin activated his shipwide commlink node to speak to the crew while he sat in the captain's chair. "All hands. This is the Captain. We are returning to continue our exploration of the Baidam Constellation, which, as we learned from our last trip, was once called the Big Dipper back on Earth.

"Our mission remains substantially the same. Search for the Lost Colonies and conduct detailed surveys of the systems we encounter along the way. While we are out in deep space, we'll be on our own and

Cerberus will depend upon each of you to do your jobs as best you can and trust your shipmates to do the same. Ronin out."

No one spoke while Perez maneuvered the big ship away from Wayside Station. About a half hour later, he interrupted the silence by announcing, "We've cleared the minimum safe distance, Captain. Ready to jump the ship."

Ronin glanced at Mueller, who was now standing next to him. She smiled and raised her eyebrows as if to say, "Well, what are you waiting for?" Her look caused Ronin to snort a small laugh, then he nodded towards Perez at the Helm Station. "Mr. Perez, jump the ship."

Breaking into a big smile, Perez responded enthusiastically as he turned to his screens and instruments. "Aye, aye, jump the ship!"

Moments later, Cerberus vanished in a small jump flare.

After the ship reappeared, Ronin looked to Lieutenant Delacroix and asked, "Lieutenant, what's our position?"

Delacroix was already checking his scans. "Taking readings now, Captain."

Approximately 20 seconds elapsed while everyone on the bridge turned to look at Delacroix expectantly. It was taking so much longer than normal.

"Captain, we crossed 20 light years from Sol system in that single jump! We're well on the way to the Baidam Constellation," Delacroix finally reported.

"Very well, since we are on course to a far more distant star this time, we'll begin our navigational scanning and mapping here. Lieutenant Delacroix, it's your show now," Ronin responded.

"Aye, aye, Captain. Beginning long range scans now," Delacroix replied immediately.

Ronin stood and turned to Mueller. "Commander, I'll be in my ready room. You have the Bridge."

"Aye, Captain, I have the Bridge," Mueller promptly responded.

***

Dan Ronin danced away from his attacker's right foot as it whipped past his face in a lightening quick wheelhouse kick, timing his own counter to skip forward a small step to launch a left roundhouse into his opponent's face that inevitably had been following the foot around a little bit. Ronin pulled the kick back slightly, letting the foot pad protecting the top of his kicking leg's foot make a slightly jarring contact with Gunnery Sgt. Brett Blackwater's face.

Blackwater grunted his displeasure at taking the bait so poorly and exposing himself to Ronin's well-timed counter kick. He was feeling aggressive today, which is always dangerous for the sparring partner of a second-degree black belt in tae kwon do, but Ronin was no slouch in the sport. Ronin himself was a third-degree black belt in tae kwon do, a fighting style that was rumored to have originated more than three thousand years ago.

The two longtime sparring partners continued to look for openings inside the sparring ring. Ronin was doing his bobbing-and-weaving-to-the-side-thing that drove Blackwater nuts. That meant he was constantly circling to the left or right, just fast enough to throw off an attacker's timing and aim, but not so fast as to tire himself out.

Both of them threw a few kick combinations every time they attacked, but the auto-scorers built into their pads only registered three clean hits to the midsection plus Ronin's head kick on Blackwater. Ronin was leading four points to one, since the head kick counted for two points.

Just when Ronin figured he had an opening to Blackwater's upper chest, he skipped forward with an axe kick thrown by his front leg to save time. Ronin's heel flew up over Blackwater's backside and left shoulder before impacting the left side, upper chest on the way down. Blackwater's hand's had been guarding too low to stop the clever move.

The two were trying to break apart to keep sparring when an annoying face appeared in Ronin's vision. Blackwater and Ronin were so startled by the unexpected interruption, they lost their footing and collapsed into a painful heap on the floor.

"Captain!" said Dr. Wright loudly. "I've been trying to get your attention!" the man said impatiently. With graying hair and of medium build with a small potbelly that he tried to hide by wearing tweed vests, Dr. Wright was the civilian Protocol Office onboard Cerberus and leader of the small diplomatic corps. Originating from the reforested wilderness of what was once called "Massachusetts", Wright thought of himself as eminent and distinguished looking and he habitually reminded everyone to use his educational title of "Dr." None of the ship's crew agreed with Wright's high opinion of himself.

Blackwater groaned and rumbled his displeasure at falling to the ground in a tangled pile of limbs. It was the best they could do to avoid accidentally causing serious injury to Wright and to each other, thanks to Wright's unwise interruption in the middle of an active sparring match.

"*Dr.* Wright, you EVER stick your face in the middle of a sparring match again, I will take a personal interest in seeing that unspeakable things happen to you!" Blackwater growled, emphasizing the man's title, while Ronin extracted himself from the tangle. Ronin was also glaring angrily at Wright.

"Captain, I ..." Wright began to say, but Ronin cut him off.

"Dr. Wright. I assume you fail to appreciate how narrowly we escaped serious injury just now, so I will educate you. I nearly delivered a knee to your head, and Gunnery Sergeant Blackwater nearly clocked you with a counterpunch that he threw at me before you appeared.

"Given that either would have been sufficient to break an inch or two of oak wood, you would have been badly hurt had either connected with you. Instead, we risked serious injury to avoid injuring you. Do that again, and you will end up cleaning the head for the duration of this mission."

"Nonsense, Captain. I'm sure you have some new yeomen to perform the menial labor on Cerberus. We need to discuss my new plans for updating the First Contact protocols and you haven't returned my messages," Wright said breezily.

Stunned, Blackwater gaped at Wright. It occurred to Blackwater that Wright would probably just misinterpret his reaction as Neanderthal-like drooling and mouth breathing instead of shock so he just as quickly shut his mouth again.

Ronin stood up to his full height, his eyes furious. "*Dr.* Wright," he said icily. "Few details would bring me more pleasure than to assign you, and only you, to clean the ship's crappers with a toothbrush.

"I will get back to your messages when I return them. Make no mistake. As Captain it is MY prerogative to do so at a time and priority that is convenient to me. I do not find the time to be convenient as this is my exercise period. Now return to your post, and await my reply."

For once, the self-important Dr. Wright realized the better part of discretion was simply to nod and reply, "As you wish, Captain Ronin," before leaving the gym.

Blackwater's eyebrows shot up as he glanced from Wright's retreating backside back to Ronin. "You want I should arrange for the good doctor to learn from these educational moments, Captain?"

Ronin's mouth formed a half-smile, but it was cold and without mirth as his eyes met Blackwater's. "Don't tempt me like that, Gunny. I'm a weak man."

Blackwater snorted before resuming his fighting stance. "Let's finish this, 'cause you're an old man. Time for you to get that beating you so richly deserve."

Ronin's short laugh echoed off the walls. "Keep talking, cupcake, keep talking," he replied, and he, too, raised his hands to assume his fighting stance again.

CHAPTER 4

THE JUNGLE

The young teenager stepped softly as he padded down the heavily shaded trail. The weather was stifling. At least 115 degrees Fahrenheit at the height of the day, and humidity thick enough to feel like a person needed gills to breathe.

Sweat poured off him as his eyes tried to find a threat to their owner's well-being in this mess. The Jungle was a riot of unfamiliar tropical plants, movement, and wildlife sounds. With danger seemingly lurking everywhere, Seth Galruud employed all the hunting and survival techniques he had learned from the elder warriors of his Faction in his small village hidden up in the cold mountains of Ullr. The powerfully built 15-year-old had learned well as his eyes continued to track the paw prints of a Hellcat.

Galruud's mind kept rehearsing what he learned about Hellcats before embarking on his hunting Sojourn, that rite of passage undertaken by all able-bodied tribal males, as well as any females choosing the warrior life. A Sojourner was a 15-year-old who was trained to fight with the weapon of elite warriors, the Monosabre, which is a double-sided long sword blade with an incredibly sharp monofilament edge that easily cuts through most everything but hull plating. Galruud didn't fully understand the science of why a monofilament blade could cut through most materials with little resistance, but he certainly respected its awesome power.

A Hellcat, Galruud had been taught, was a large, genetically improved Bengal tiger. When the first colonists arrived on this planet, they had brought the original tiger DNA with them to breed and serve as a hunter of an indigenous predator. That predator was a large, powerful lizard that had killed most of the original tigers. That lizard's prowess at killing humans and tigers eventually prompted the colonists to create a genetically improved apex predator from the tiger DNA, which they called the Hellcat.

Galruud knew the new breed of Hellcats hunted their prey into extinction in just over a century, and that they were still intelligent enough to escape their captivity and replace the lizards as the new apex predator. The only thing that seemed to limit their range was the Hellcat's inability to cross into the dry, desert regions where most of the human populations live. Most, except for Galruud's Faction. The Ullr, and the cold, northern continent from which the Ullrians took their name, shared a small land bridge that extended far to the south into the Jungle climate zone. During warmer months, Hellcats hunted their prey as far north as they dared before returning to the Jungle to escape the winter weather.

In his mind's eye Galruud replayed the lessons his father taught him. "Hellcats are highly intelligent. They're much stronger than the Bengal tiger, can range further, hunt more quietly, and have claws and teeth that their new genetics made stronger than steel. Track them quietly, always check behind you, and be wary because they can jump at least twenty feet high to get at you in a tree. Three out of four Sojourners never return," Galruud Sr. had told him one night over a campfire.

Three out of four never return, Galruud thought to himself as he silently tracked the prints down the game trail while his hands held his weapon ready. He used to think scornfully about the Sojourners who never returned, believing them to have been flawed, lesser beings. Now that he was out here all by himself, the omnipresent dangers and "survival-of-the-fittest" vibe of the Jungle had rapidly disabused Galruud of such childish notions.

Galruud followed the prints for a couple of hundred yards before they suddenly appeared to be deeper. Stooping to look more closely, Seth determined the Hellcat had paused here to observe something without moving to avoid attracting attention to itself. Its sheer weight, held motionless in one spot for a while, caused the prints to be deeper.

Unbidden, a thought sprang into his mind. *Probably watching its own prey.*

Sweat continued to roll down his sides in rivulets in the steamy heat. Galruud stayed hydrated by drinking from the streams he passed as he continued pursuing his quarry. This deep into the Jungle, only a few small beams of light stabbed down through gaps in the thick canopy formed by the trees. It didn't seem strange to Seth to see a rain forest of Amazonian-derived trees on this colony. Or that the Jungle, as the population of this world called it, was located in a tropical band on a hot planet where you would normally find the temperate band on Earth. It's just the way it was here, and it had been that way for hundreds of years.

An hour passed, somehow seeming to pass both quickly due to the danger, and slowly due to the harsh Jungle environment. His senses hyper alert despite fatigue, Galruud suddenly noticed how quiet it had become. The background symphony of animal noises had disappeared, leaving only the soft rustling of leaves up in the canopy from a wispy breeze that didn't reach the floor of the Jungle.

A Hellcat is near, Galruud thought, recalling that the wildlife in the Jungle goes silent when they realize one is in the area. He quickly checked his gear and the area behind him to make sure he wasn't about to get jumped from behind. The prints continued ahead, deeper now due to their freshness as well as the wet, vaguely spongy soil. Fresh tracks. Galruud crept ahead more slowly now, trying to see and hear in every direction at the same time.

Suddenly, a shrill scream broke the relative calm, nearly causing Galruud to faint from terror and adrenaline. The animal scream was swiftly cut short, and Galruud could hear the sounds of a massive animal tearing the flesh of its prey.

He crouched and took a few more steps to approach a small hill so he could peek cautiously over the top. There it was, feeding. A Hellcat. About two thousand pounds of genetically enhanced muscle and violence, wrapped in a dark orange hide adorned with camouflaging black stripes. The huge beast stopped its feeding frenzy of an antelope-like creature, sniffing the air.

Galruud suddenly was horrified to see the creature turn its head to look at him, still sniffing. He scrambled back as quietly as he could to a large tree that was close by and pulled his Monosabre from its sheath while standing with his back to the tree. Seconds later, he could see the huge head of the Hellcat rising above the small hill on the trail to look at him. *Thank goodness they normally hunt singly and not in packs!* Galruud thought to himself as he balanced himself, ready to defend himself by attacking or moving out of the way.

A low growl started somewhere deep inside the Hellcat. The sound stunned Galruud and seemed to shake the very ground. It promised violence and anger, and the depth of its bass vibrations caused a palpable shiver of fear in every living being within earshot.

The Hellcat decided that merely growling wasn't sufficient, breaking into a truly impressive roar that would have shamed its genetic ancestors with its sheer animal violence. The King of the Jungle was going to eat well today.

Galruud pointed his Monosabre at the giant Hellcat and announced, "I... am not afraid of you, cat." He couldn't have been more surprised by its reply.

"Humaaaaan," the giant Hellcat said in its gravelly voice. "Diiiieeeee," it rumbled, drawing the word out in a ghastly manner as it crouched in preparation to leap at its new prey.

Galruud's blood turned ice cold at being talked to by this thing, and he now knew what fear truly was.

CHAPTER 5

MIDDLE OF NOWHERE

"**S**omehow, I had expected deep space exploration in a famous warship like Cerberus to be, I dunno, a bit more glamorous?" grumbled Leroy Greene, the junior protocol officer, as he sat in the ship's otherwise empty mess hall with his elbows on the dining table and hands clasping a steaming cup of Navy coffee in front of his face. A proud alumnus of the Diplomatic Institute of North America, Greene was a fresh replacement for Prisha Gadre, who had made first contact with Terra Station. Gadre had chosen to remain on that colony after the Cargo Rebellion to serve as Earth's ambassador. She had her hands full managing the diplomatic relations between the two worlds.

"The mission to Terra Station took quite awhile too, Leroy. This ship is mapping out the routes and looking for navigational hazards along the way. It takes a lot of time," cautioned Dr. Winston Wright to his young protégé. "The crew is very dedicated. Let them do their jobs without making things more difficult."

Greene's face failed to hide his annoyance at having to wait around for these uneducated rubes to draw space maps with their crayons. A child of privilege, Greene grew up in a very wealthy, exclusive enclave on the Atlantic coast in South Carolina. His perfect, pearly white teeth contrasted with his nearly coal black skin and curly hair. "I don't understand why the Captain doesn't just jump us all the way to our destination. Why doesn't someone explain this ship's capabilities to him? The man only seems to understand how to shoot things."

Even Wright's eyebrows shot up at the cluelessness of Greene's remark. He paused a moment to collect his thoughts before responding. "Leroy, you're complaining about the most famous person on Earth, doing the job he's been given, and doing it better than anybody. While you stayed safe and sound at your parent's mansion and taking classes at a prestigious private school, this Captain and crew sacrificed just about everything to fight and win a brutal war for Earth. Now they've won another war on Terra Station. Anyone on this crew hears you grumble like that about him, the crew, or this ship, and they'll eat you alive."

Greene just shook his head softly. "But they don't know what they're doing. They just have training given to them by the Navy or the Marines," he retorted.

"Yes, I know. And yet, here they are, victorious and going back to deep space again. I thought the same way before the last mission, and have realized I was wrong. I don't have a good handle on the nuances of acting as a member of a crew instead of a faculty member, but I'm trying to learn before the Captain decides enough is enough and leaves me on a distant rock somewhere.

"I suggest you try to get over thinking that university learning is more valuable than learning from experience. If you don't, you'll just cause problems here," Wright cautioned. He hoped the young man would start to unlearn his prejudices before it was too late. Problems in space tend to get people killed.

Green sighed and raised his eyebrows. He found it hard to believe Dr. Wright was speaking to him this way, so he decided to mollify him to get him to shut up. "If you say so. It's pretty galling to be bossed around by a bunch of sailors, but I'll follow your lead."

Just then, Commander Mueller walked through the hatchway into the mess with her husband, Dr. Karl Mueller. *At least HE has a proper education*, thought Greene as he stood up to greet them.

"Commander, Dr. Mueller. Uh, hi. Um, is there anything I can help either of you with while we're charting the area?" Greene asked. He would at least try to give the appearance of trying to be helpful.

The Muellers shared a glance at each other. The only thing faster than the FTL jump drive on Cerberus was the gossip and rumors among the ship's crew. Cerberus left Wayside Station three months prior and had spent the entire time charting space. That was plenty of time for the

Mueller's to hear rumors about Leroy Greene's superior, snobbish attitude towards the rest of the crew. By now, the crew avoided the young man, or worse, played small practical jokes on him. Not enough to get themselves in hack, but enough to make the annoying youngster believe space travel was beneath his dignity and training.

Aware that this conversation fell under Diane's realm of responsibility, Karl let her do the talking. Shaking her head slightly, Commander Mueller smiled and responded, "Mr. Greene, I don't believe the current part of the mission would be a good fit for someone with your highly specialized skill set. Hopefully we'll encounter a colony and you'll be plenty busy then."

Nodding his head, Green said, "Thank you, Commander. If you'll excuse me then, I'll return to the protocol office." *Thank goodness they didn't want my help with their menial little jobs*, Green thought to himself as he walked through the mess hatchway into the corridor beyond.

Nodding a greeting to Dr. Wright and receiving one in return, the Muellers grabbed mugs of coffee and found a quiet table in the far corner where no one could hear them, including Dr. Wright.

"Highly specialized skill set?" Karl asked, doing a poor job of hiding his amused half-smile.

Diane chuckled and sipped her coffee. Somehow managing to have a perfectly straight face, she responded to Karl, "Normally, I'd stick a clueless kid like that on a work detail where he couldn't cause any harm. But nobody wants to get stuck with him. And I mean that literally. NOBODY," she said, softly emphasizing that last word.

"Dan and I already discussed what to do with him. We concluded that buttering him up was the best solution, because he's gullible enough to believe it. Flattery reinforces Greene's own misguided prejudices and biases, and keeps him right where he's at. He's Dr. Wright's problem unless it gets worse. Even looking past his demeanor issues and big head, the kid hasn't acquired any skills that would be valuable aboard a ship. We don't have the luxury of assigning someone to just train him to be useful."

Karl just shook his head. "Wow. With such a ringing endorsement, I don't think my area would be a good fit for him, either," he noted with a crooked smile. Obviously his team wouldn't mesh well with a clueless young diplomat whose only gift is a raging sense of entitlement.

***

He looked at his opponents, using all his skill and talent to prevent his intentions from ever reaching his eyes on a face that otherwise appeared placidly impassive. Each of the other seven eyed him with suspicion, with a small touch of fear clouding the expressions of two of them. *Are they afraid, or is that just their tells?* Lt. Pierre Delacroix wondered. The eight of them remained silent, warily waiting for the next move.

They didn't have to wait long. Lt. Cmdr. Elvis Lazarus pulled a one-eyed Jack of Spades from the cards in his hand and slowly laid it on the discard pile. "Call," he said clearly, matching the bet with the necessary number of chips in the pot.

There was a collective gasp from the Marines on their feet, surrounding the table down in Marine Country. The stakes on this hand were sky high and they had been watching the game between the eight players seated at the table. Somebody was going to make bank on this hand.

The players who hadn't already folded laid their cards down one at a time. Lazarus laid down his hand first. "Straight," he said simply, a bead of sweat having appeared on his forehead. His hand showed five cards in sequential order, a respectable hand.

All eyes flicked to Cpl. Adrian Longman, sitting to Lazarus' left. With a suspicious glance at Delacroix, he showed his hand. "Flush," he said, causing the other Marines who were watching to politely whistle and whoop for one of their own, but they weren't willing to cut loose and declare Longman the winner because Delacroix hadn't shown his cards yet.

Dr. Karl Mueller laid down his cards. "Two pair." Although Mueller's face showed disappointment at not being able to conjure up a better hand this time, he had collected the tidy sum of chips in front of him by playing well tonight.

Two more players simply showed their cards, both saying, "I'm out." Each of their hands held only two pairs.

Still looking impassive, Delacroix laid down his hand. "Four of a kind," he said, only raising his eyebrows to acknowledge another huge poker victory, while the crowd of Marine onlookers roared. Money began changing hands between the men and women in the crowd to pay off their individual side bets on who would win the game.

As the players gathered their winnings and the gambling paraphernalia was stowed to be used at another time for another high stakes game, Delacroix quietly sidled up to Lieutenant Gustav. "Well played, once again, Pierre!" Gustav said with a grin as his side bet on Delacroix paid off handsomely.

"Thanks, Adolph. Thought Mueller had me at the end this time," Delacroix replied, now allowing himself to grin. He handed Gustav half of the winnings. "Here's a little contribution for the Recreational Fund. Keep our people in good stead." As he said this, Mueller likewise passed half of his winnings over as well.

Gustav's smile grew broader. He caught the eye of Gunnery Sgt. Toshi Kanagawa and motioned him over.

"Sir?" asked Kanagawa moments later.

"Gunny, this is Delacroix and Mueller's latest donations to the Recreational Fund. You know what to do with it," Gustav said.

Kanagawa's smile lit up the room. "Oh, yessirs!" he replied, drawling the words together as was common on Cerberus. "The Marines thank you for another important contribution towards crew morale."

Kanagawa saluted the two lieutenants and clapped Mueller on his shoulder. Then he quickly shoved off to go and secure the money. Delacroix and Mueller had heavily added to the fund several times during this expedition, although it was Delacroix who was currently on a huge winning streak. While he was relatively new to the poker table down in Marine Country, Mueller was a decent player and had quickly adopted Delacroix's custom of regularly contributing half of his winnings to the fund. Their habit of heavy contributions had made them favorites among the side bettors who watched the festivities.

Delacroix just smiled as he watched Kanagawa, secure in the knowledge that donating half of the winnings he doesn't need anyway will keep getting him seats at the poker table.

CHAPTER 6

CORA NOSTRA

"**W**ell? How bad are they hurting us?" grumbled Don Morelino after taking a puff on his cigar. His piercing blue eyes narrowed slightly as he looked intently down the large table towards Duke Lordano, the Morelino family consigliere.

Lordano cleared his throat slightly, while Don Morelino waited for his reply impatiently and swirled the bourbon in the whiskey glass that replaced the cigar in his right hand.

"It's bad," said Lordano. "They hijacked our ship's cargo with the load of diamonds and gold on it. Estimated value of the cargo alone was 10 million credits. The missing ship was worth about 15 million. Factor in the surviving family member payments to spouses and such, total losses are over 30 million."

Morelino knew it was bad, but this was worse news than he had steeled himself to receive. "Thirty MILLION?" he exploded. The other men seated at the table remained very quiet, smartly not wanting to draw attention to themselves while Morelino processed the bad news. "Why didn't our security stop them?'

"Because they're dead. And we have a good idea on who did it, too," Lordano added, angrily. "Analysis of their drive exhaust matches the drive signatures of those damned Ullrians and their raiding ships."

Lordano knew that identifying Ullrians as the attackers also explained why the crew and security for the missing ship were dead. Their warrior ethos demanded they slay all enemy combatants, but for differing reasons. Those trying to surrender offended the Ullrians maniacal sense of honor, so they were simply executed as unworthy. Those who chose to fight had to fight to the death or win, but at least they might be regarded by Ullrians as an honorable opponent if they fought well.

"I really hate those crazy killers. Do we know where our ship is now?" Morelino asked.

Lordano shook his head. "No. They found and disabled all our tracking and positioning devices. The last we saw of our ship was some unknown vessel towing it into the Ullrian part of the asteroid belt at high speed. We'll never hear from it again."

Morelino sighed, mostly out of exasperation but somewhat out of weariness, too. "OK. Duke, tell our guys, they see anybody they don't like out there, they have carte blanche to take them out as they see fit. Meanwhile, we gotta hit the Ullrians, and hit them hard. I wanna see your plans on that over dinner tomorrow, understand?" Morelino said, jabbing the index finger of his hand that was again holding the cigar towards Lordano for emphasis.

"I do, Don Morelino. We've got some ideas to make them hurt," Lordano promised.

CHAPTER 7

DEEP SPACE

"**W**hat if we don't find anything this time? We've been searching for seven months now," said Lazarus over a steaming mug of coffee he was holding in front of his face as he rested his elbows on the table in an otherwise empty break room.

"Is that so bad? We've greatly expanded our stellar cartography data banks this trip. And no one has been shooting at us this whole exploration trip, either," replied Lt. Marcy Anzio.

Lazarus snorted softly before taking a sip. "From an engineering perspective, it turns out exploration isn't as exciting as I imagined."

Anzio smiled and laughed softly, before taking a sip of her coffee. "At least you have to keep an eye on the ship's systems to make sure they're all running within the proper parameters. I've been stuck running simulations and performing other duties because there's nothing to shoot at."

"What's the next system we're going to investigate?" Lazarus asked.

"Alioth. It's the brightest star in the Baidam Constellation, which is the constellation we had barely begun to investigate during the Terra Station trip," Anzio answered.

Lazarus nodded. "Baidam Constellation. That's the constellation also known on Terra Station by the old name, the Big Dipper, and also is part of the Ursa Major Constellation. Did I get it right?"

Anzio nodded. "Yep. This trip out we were given a few different systems to check out before we arrived back at the Constellation. We haven't discovered any more Lost Colonies, but Lieutenant Delacroix says we have discovered massive reserves of natural resources."

Lazarus looked thoughtful for a moment before asking, "Do any of the systems we've looked at look like good prospects for colonization?"

Anzio shook her head. "No. Nothing promising. Not even with the pre-Fall terraforming technology that we obtained from the poles at Terra Station."

"Resource mining stations then, if we ever put any facilities in those systems. Sounds like a heavily automated, grim and lonely existence," Lazarus noted.

"Ha!" laughed Anzio. "They pay well enough, and somebody will agree to work those sites just on that basis alone."

CHAPTER 8

FOXTROT STATION

"**W**e are now at Foxtrot Station. Distance to Alioth System, approximately 15 light years, Captain," announced Delacroix from the scanning station. "No contacts detected, no celestial bodies in our vicinity."

"Tacnet reports no threats, Captain," added Lt. Matt LeCroy from his tactical station. Tacnet hadn't reported any threats for months.

Ronin nodded in acknowledgment and opened a commlink. "Lieutenant Sunderland, this is the Captain. We're at Foxtrot Station. You're a go for launch."

"Aye, Captain. Go for launch," came Sunderland's crisp response.

Sunderland opened a commlink to his Bulldog crews. "Bulldog crews, we're at Foxtrot Station. Launch your birds."

A chorus of confirmation replies flooded Sunderland's commlink, and moments later the ship shuddered ever so slightly with the departure of the Bulldogs from their launch tubes.

Each of the black shuttles jumped away soon after launching.

***

"Anything?" asked Pilot Officer Erin Johnson. She was beyond bored as her shuttle, Bulldog 1, drifted along in space. Her Alabama accent clearly conveyed her unspoken message to hustle it up.

Her rearseater, Chief Hal Patterson, sighed before replying in his deep Texas drawl. "I got miles and miles of nothing but empty miles. Area scans are nearly complete and we can jump to the next point in a few minutes."

The minutes crawled by before Patterson's instruments finished. He looked at the readouts. "Random dust particles. Some unusual energy readings, nothing special though. I'm sending you the coordinates for the next jump."

Johnson snorted softly. At last there was something to do now that Patterson sent the next jump coordinates. "Spinning up the jump engines now. Jumping in three. Two. One. Jump!"

Bulldog 1 jumped away with a tiny jump flare. It unexpectedly reappeared with a large jump flare, radiating away large amounts of energy in all directions.

"Mis-jump!" yelled Johnson over the blare of several different internal alarms. The Bulldog was juddering from some sort of external force. "What the heck happened?"

"I dunno! I don't even know where we are yet!" Patterson yelled back. His hands were rapidly operating his boards. The juddering stopped while he was distracted.

"Taking a navigational reading now," Patterson said, calmer now. "That can't be right!" he exclaimed loudly a few moments later.

"What?" Johnson asked, turning to look at Patterson.

Patterson looked at Johnson, his eyes wide. "We're a little beyond the outer edge of the Alioth system."

"WHAT!" Johnson exclaimed, putting a whole different emphasis on the same word. "How can that be? Bulldogs can't jump more than a light year at a time."

"I know!" Patterson exclaimed. Just as he was about to say something else, a new alarm on his system demanded his attention. "Contact astern! Distance, 500,000 miles. Getting more scan returns now. Object matches no known configurations."

"I'm spinning up the engines for an emergency jump," Johnson announced as she began reaching for the controls.

"Wait! We don't know what happened or if it's safe to jump again," Patterson said. "And the object doesn't appear to be moving relative to anything in the system. It's stationary."

Johnson pulled her hand back from the jump drive controls. "Five hundred thousand miles is pretty close. If the object launches any missiles towards us, I won't have much time to jump the ship away."

Patterson continued to receive more information from his scans, and put an image of the object up on his main screen and Johnson's screen. They both stared at it in quiet shock for a few moments. "It's definitely not a naturally occurring object," commented Patterson.

Their screens digitally projected the outline of a hollow ring. As he read from his scans, Patterson said, "It's too far away to see with the naked eye. Our AI is estimating its interior diameter at 100 miles across, and the ring is approximately a mile thick. Readings suggest it's some sort of metal alloy of unknown composition. AI indicates whatever alloy that is, it must be significantly stronger than any alloy we know of. Color is matte black, so it will be very difficult to see even up close. No energy signature either, or at least none of that we can recognize."

"Hal," Johnson said, using Patterson's first name. "I think we need to look more closely. Do you agree?"

Patterson nodded as the two turned to look at each other. "Yeah. Our message drones can be launched into the system from here to carry an update for Cerberus in case something happens to us."

"It's too bad we don't have drones with jump drives yet," Johnson muttered. "That would be handy."

"Too many competing priorities to have had enough time to make small jump-capable drones that a Bulldog can haul. I heard the Captain sweet-talked Naval Intelligence into rigging up a Bulldog with an AI, a jump drive and a drone package so we can call home for help or send a message. But that's too big for a crewed Bulldog to use," Patterson replied. A few seconds later, he added, "I've loaded up our message drone with our logs and data. Ready for launch."

Johnson answered immediately. "Launch drone."

There was a slight thump as the drone detached from the bottom of the Bulldog. "Drone away," Patterson said.

"I'm going to take us closer to the ring," Johnson said, distracted now that she was laying in the course.

***

In space floated the huge, matte black ring. It seemingly hung motionless against a starry background, and was difficult to see due to its non-reflective color and weak light this far from Alioth. "No sign of other ships so far, but there seems to be a thin ring of asteroids out here," said Patterson. His eyes were glued to his screens as he tried to plot any hazards to their well-being out here.

"Asteroids? Way out here?" Johnson asked as she slowed down the Bulldog as a precaution. "Those are usually much closer to the sun in a system," she noted.

"Yeah, but that's based on our observations of a sample size of less than ten star systems, in total," Patterson replied. "Pretty small sample for a pretty big galaxy."

"Well, there's that," Johnson said sheepishly.

"These rocks are uniformly radioactive. More than the ambient radiation out here," Patterson noted.

"A danger to us?" Johnson asked.

"Keep us at a safe distance. They're hot enough to cause us problems if we try to park on one," Patterson said.

Lost in their thoughts, the Bulldog flew on for several more minutes, until the ring loomed large in their window.

"I'm not picking up any details on our scans beyond the overall size of this monster," Patterson said after double checking his instruments.

"Nothing? Not even a... a hanger door or something?" Johnson asked.

"Absolutely nothing. It's like it only partially exists in this universe. No power signature. No ambient temperature. No radiation. No communications. No doorways or airlocks. Nothing at all," Patterson said, as he turned to look at Johnson.

"That's not possible!" Johnson exclaimed as she glanced back out the front canopy towards the giant structure.

"Yet it's right in front of us. And we're both wondering if this thing brought us here out of our jump," Patterson commented, saying what they'd both been thinking.

"Can we find this thing again if we leave?" Johnson asked, cocking an eyebrow at Patterson.

"We have detailed coordinate readings marked now. We'll be able to find it again unless it moves. The real question is whether we'll be able to move ..." Patterson trailed off.

"Let's try it and see," Johnson muttered. "Setting coordinates for a light week from our current position, straight towards the system. Ready?"

"Ready," Patterson said distractedly as he worked his instruments to take careful recordings of as much data as he could.

Bulldog 1 disappeared in a small jump flare and reappeared closer into the system.

"Taking a nav reading now ..." Patterson said as his voice trailed off, providing a commentary on what he was doing. "We're a light week closer to the star. Right where we're supposed to be."

Patterson and Johnson traded confused looks. "Jump back and try another?" Johnson asked, somewhat rhetorically.

Patterson nodded, eyebrows raised now.

The Bulldog reappeared 500,000 miles from the ring, with a large jump flare and radiating away large amounts of energy in all directions again.

"Wait! I set the coordinates for where we jumped away from, not 500,000 miles out!" Johnson noted with confusion.

"We're in the exact same place we arrived at the first time." Patterson noted. "We fell out of our jump the same way, too."

"I don't get what's happening!" Johnson said.

"I have a suspicion. Let's jump away and back at decreasing angles from the ring." Patterson said.

Johnson turned and looked at him. "You think this thing is influencing a set area of space?"

Patterson nodded at her. "I do. My theory is this thing acts like a trap to bring ships here so they can use the gate for longer jumps."

"BIG assumption," Johnson snorted, emphasizing the first word.

Patterson was undeterred. "Clearly. But what if this actually IS a jump gate? And jump drives were just meant for short hops in a system instead of interstellar travel like we're using them for?"

Surprised, Johnson just looked at him for a moment. "That ... actually would make sense." She turned back to her instruments. "OK. Setting a new jump pattern following your suggestion."

The Bulldog jumped away again.

CHAPTER 9

RAIDER NO. 16

"**C**losing to within weapons range now, Captain," announced the Raider's tactical officer, Tommy Votto.

"Any sign we've been spotted?" asked Joey Saldano, captain of Raider No. 16.

The tactical officer shook his head, not taking his eyes from the screens in front of him. Turning his head slightly towards Saldano, who was seated behind him and to his right, Votto vocalized his opinion. "Negative. No change in target aspect. It doesn't appear as if they expected to get hit from the thickest part of the asteroid belt."

Saldano snorted and glanced around the small bridge. There were only four of them who could squeeze into the small, dimly lit compartment, and there was no room to stand up and stretch without getting in someone else's way.

Comms Officer Jeanie Crespi announced, "Target is still radio silent."

"Give me a countdown until max firing range," ordered Saldano. He leaned forward in his chair, staring intently at the main view screen.

Votto put the timer on the lower right corner of the main view screen. It was counting down from 33 seconds.

No one spoke as their small raiding ship continued to maneuver through the asteroid field. The 33 seconds passed quickly.

"Range?" Saldano asked.

Votto was ready for the question. "Currently within our max range at 100,000 kilometers now. Target is still stationery. Closure rate is 100 kilometers per minute."

Saldano decided that was close enough. "Tommy, you are cleared to fire at your discretion. As soon as Tommy launches, I want Eddie to do a full burn to get us clear and back into the thickest part of the asteroid field. Everybody clear on that?"

As was common in the small Cosa Nostra Raiders, Saldano tended to use names instead of ranks when addressing the crew. There weren't enough of them to stand on rank, and their living situation was so cramped it tended to encourage the informality.

"Engines ready for full burn on Votto's signal," reported the ship's pilot, Eddie Vega, which was his way of confirming his readiness to execute the maneuver. Eddie wasn't known for saying much.

About another minute passed in silence before it was broken by Votto. "Targeting solution entered into the weapons guidance systems. Receipt confirmed. Preparing to fire," he said, verbally walking the bridge crew through the steps he was taking.

More seconds passed. The silence now broken only by the sounds of the small ship.

Votto didn't need to announce when the missiles launched. Raider No. 16 was small enough that they could all feel jolts as they sprang from their firing tubes.

Votto resumed his commentary. "All birds away! Tracking straight and true. Ullrian defense systems just activated."

Just as he finished, Votto's voice trailed off with the strain from the suddenly increased Gs as Raider No. 16 engaged its main engines. The small ship's gravity compensator wasn't quite up to the task of offsetting the Gs caused by the tight turn and thrust. The small Raider class of the Cosa Nostra was outfitted with extremely powerful engines and maneuvering thrusters. So overpowered were the little ships that Saldano tended to consider them little more than giant engines and weapons pods strapped to a small hull. *We can deliver a hit, but we sure can't take one*, Saldano thought to himself while the breath was being slowly squeezed out of him. Saldano often thought that during hard turns and burns. The Raiders' high maneuverability came at a high cost as they had little armor to slow them down.

The acceleration Gs fell back below the threshold where the gravity compensator could overcome their effects on the crew as the Raider reached what Saldano felt was a reasonable escape velocity. Soon after they could breathe again, Votto's voice commanded everyone's attention.

"Impact! Multiple impacts! It appears the Ullrian longship was destroyed! Looks like significant damage to the base and mining operations on the asteroid." Votto announced, his voice betraying his excitement at the success of the raid. He was staring hard at the video feed on his personal screen from the ship's long range telescopes.

Whoops and whistles from the bridge crew followed that announcement. As he listened to his crew's small celebration, Saldano couldn't help but start brooding about the future. *All this. And for what? The Ullrians ALWAYS strike back*, he thought. It was a sobering thought.

CHAPTER 10

CERBERUS

"**F**ood stocks are continuing to dwindle. Currently, we have roughly three months' supply left. Water recycling is at peak efficiency. And Doc Taketa reports our stores of medicines and medical supplies are good because there's been few injuries or events requiring their use," Mueller said to Ronin as they sat at a quiet table in a corner of the mess hall. She paused to take a sip of her steaming mug of coffee, then looked down at it appreciatively. "Ah! This must be the good stuff from your contraband coffee stash. Sure tastes better than that vile stuff the Navy serves."

Ronin poured himself a mug of coffee from the thermos he brought along to the mess hall. It was brewed from the illicit cache of Kona beans he smuggled aboard before they departed. It was a little gift from Admiral Rodding, who was well aware of Ronin's love of Kona coffee. He smiled evilly as he closed up the thermos and set it on the table. "I think it's the Navy's theory that there is some sort of sliding scale of direct correlation between foul-tasting coffee and crew efficiency."

"Something like crew efficiency rises in direct correlation to the awfulness of the coffee?" Mueller snorted a soft laugh and took another sip.

Ronin nodded, a half-smile on his face. "Yup. And the irony that I bring my own brew must somehow correlate to poor efficiency under the Navy's theory hasn't escaped me."

A louder laugh escaped from Mueller. She would have looked around to check whether anyone overheard, but she could see the mess hall was empty from where she sat.

Ronin's face grew more serious. "We're going to need to address our food situation soon. Unless we find something we can turn into nutrition, we will have to return home for resupply."

It was Mueller's turn to nod. "Agreed. We haven't found too many grocery stores out here. And we can't just order up some take out ..." Her voice trailed off as her attention was diverted by the arrival of Lt. Kristoff Alphonso, who ran the ship's Fabrication unit.

"Captain, Commander," Alphonso said, nodding his head in greeting. "That's not Navy coffee, is it?" he asked with raised eyebrows and a hopeful tone of voice. He held a mug in his hands.

Ronin snorted and cracked a smile. "Maybe-ish. Who's asking?" he replied, stretching out the "maybe."

"Just a poor guy who's hoping to be hooked up with the good stuff to celebrate a little bit," Alphonso said, in a tone both hopeful and humorous.

"Celebrate? Do tell!" Mueller said.

Ronin nodded for Alphonso to grab a seat and filled Alphonso's mug.

"Since it's been a quiet cruise so far, the mad scientists in Fabrication have been hard at work trying to noodle out the intricacies of the energy weapons we obtained from Terra Station. We finally figured it all out, and we can power it using the ship's engines," Alphonso announced, before triumphantly taking a sip of the Kona coffee. "Oh, geez! That IS the good stuff!" he said appreciatively.

"Really?" Ronin asked. "Can we bolt one of those rayguns onto the hull and find a handy power outlet where we can plug it in somewhere?"

Alphonso shook his head. "Not exactly. The intensive power cabling and couplings required to operate one involves reconfiguring a railgun turret. That's because the turret, its ordinance magazine and ammunition feeder system goes deep into the ship. This energy weapon would require using that space just to install the infrastructure to make it functional."

Ronin nodded thoughtfully. "Sounds like something to put on the wish list for the next time we pull into the shipyards at an Argo Station."

"Definitely. It'd be difficult to change a turret over without a shipyard to remove the railgun system first. The science behind how the energy weapon even works is fascinating, and becomes even more interesting when we tried to figure out how to run it from the ship's main power. We have plenty of available power to run the thing though. You want to hear about ..."

Mueller held up her hand, interrupting Alphonso.

"No, that's alright. Why don't you put a quick summary into your report instead?" Mueller asked. "The Captain and I are due back on the bridge. We're expecting the imminent return of our scouts."

Alphonso nodded, and took a sip of the coffee. "Will do. If you will excuse me then? I need to get back to Fabrication. We're still working on a new security system to prevent any more tactical acquisition of our experimental weapons by the Marines."

After Alphonso left, Ronin glanced over at Mueller with a grin. "Nice save. I thought we were going to be schooled in mad science for the next hour."

Mueller laughed quietly. "Yeah. There isn't enough coffee in the universe to get us through something like that."

Ronin looked thoughtful for a moment. "I wonder if Alphonso realizes it's impossible to perfect a security system that will prevent our Marines from tactically acquiring the new toys he's been creating?"

Mueller snorted. "If they are unable to breach Alphonso's system the first time, Lieutenant Gustav will make it his team's mission in life to find a way in there."

Their conversation was interrupted when the commlink node on Ronin's collar chimed with an incoming message.

"Captain, the Bulldogs are reappearing at the return coordinates," said Lt. Marcy Anzio, the communications officer.

"Acknowledged. Advise Lieutenant Sunderland to debrief them first and report to me after that," he replied to Anzio, then closed the commlink.

"Time to get to work," Ronin noted to Mueller.

CHAPTER 11

HADES ORDINANCE

Ronin reviewed staff reports in his ready room for a few hours. Sitting back in his seat, he rubbed his tired eyes and sighed. He wasn't bored; he had been trying to take his mind off his missing Bulldog, piloted by Erin Johnson.

They're not missing. Not quite. The six-hour return window we set as part of the scouting mission parameters hasn't been expired for too long ... yet, Ronin thought to himself. Sunderland's initial report from the Bulldog crews strongly suggested the solar system they were scouting may be populated.

Ronin decided to check in with Sunderland. He opened a commlink.

"Sunderland here. Bulldog 1 still hasn't returned, Captain," came Sunderland's voice. It wasn't the first time Ronin had asked.

"Keith, I've decided we should send out a bird to look for them if they're not back within three hours of the return window closing," Ronin said by way of greeting, using Sunderland's first name since it was just the two of them sitting in their offices.

"Way ahead of you, Captain. All the Bulldog crews have already volunteered for that duty. I tapped our glory hounds from Bulldog 3 to standby, and their bird is getting prepped and into the launch bay now."

Ronin smiled. "I knew there was a reason why you get paid the big money. We'll keep Cerberus parked here for now until we find our flight crew unless there's a better reason to relocate the ship. The science teams are going to get pretty squirrelly if we stay outside a possibly populated system much longer."

Sunderland's ears perked up at that. "Wait! You mean I'm supposed to get PAID to be the CAG? When did that start?"

Ronin snorted. "Oh yeah. We get all sorts of perks. Every paycheck's a fortune. Every meal's a banquet. Fancy clothes. Hot vehicles. It's all right in the enlistment brochure."

"Captain, I think I need to have a stern discussion with my recruiting officer. She seemed to have overlooked all those perks," Sunderland said, his voice turning serious after their banter. "I'll report back before Bulldog 3 deploys again, sir."

Ronin nodded. "Appreciate it, Keith. Ronin out."

***

Two hours later, Ronin was seated in his chair on the Bridge when Delacroix suddenly leaned forward to reread what his screen said. "Captain! Bulldog 1 just jumped back to the return point."

Almost simultaneously, Lieutenant Delgado acknowledged an incoming commlink and announced it to Ronin. "Captain, Bulldog 1 is asking for a debrief with you when they get back on board. They say they've found something."

Ronin nodded towards Delgado and replied, "Bring them home, Lieutenant, and we'll meet them in the main conference room." He looked over at Commander Mueller and lifted his eyebrows with a nod of his head to signal that he wanted her to join them.

"Aye, aye, sir," Delgado said, before passing Ronin's orders along to Bulldog 1.

The soft voice of the Cerberus AI unexpectedly filled the Bridge, causing Ronin to glance upwards at the ceiling for some reason. The AI didn't reside anyplace in Cerberus in particular. "Captain. Please be advised Bulldog 1 is now subject to the Hades Ordinance."

Every head on the Bridge turned to look at Ronin, who cocked an eyebrow. "Acknowledged. AI, please inform Lieutenant Gustav to meet us in the conference room as well."

Seconds later, the AI confirmed. "Lieutenant Gustav advises he is on his way, Captain."

"Captain, what's the Hades Ordinance?" Delgado asked.

Having joined Ronin at his chair, both Mueller and Ronin glanced at Delgado. "All I can tell you is it's a security protocol that usually leads to trouble for us, Lieutenant." Ronin stood and began to follow Mueller to leave the Bridge. "Lieutenant Delacroix, you have the Bridge."

Delacroix responded immediately. "Aye, sir. I have the Bridge."

The Bridge crew exchanged confused looks after Ronin and Mueller left. Delgado broke the silence first. "Was the Captain kidding? Or was he being serious? I couldn't tell."

As Delacroix settled into Ronin's command chair, he shook his head. "I suspect he wasn't. The Captain has a decent poker face, but I didn't get the sort of vibe that he was kidding around. Not after the AI chimed in."

Like usual, the Cerberus AI remained silent until something of sufficiently high priority required it to speak.

CHAPTER 12

LIKE OLD TIMES

"**B**ulldog 1, this is Cerberus flight control. Approach port landing bay. Auto landing approach. Speed one-nine-zero. Checker's green. Call the ball," said the ship's port landing bay flight controller over the commlink.

Before responding, Johnson quickly confirmed she had correctly aligned Bulldog 1 with the instructions before responding. "Copy that flight control. Port landing bay. Auto landing approach. Speed one-nine-zero. Checker's green. I have the ball."

As soon as navigational systems linked between Cerberus and Bulldog, Johnson activated the auto landing system and leaned back into her pilot's seat to watch the show. Cerberus' AI was now in control of Bulldog 1, and the landing went smoothly.

Bulldog 1 gently set down in the port landing bay, and its skids magnetically locked to the deck as its engines powered down. "Landing complete. Please exit for transport to the hanger deck," announced the automatic message.

Within seconds, the deck crew appeared and hooked up the Bulldog to the small towing vehicle while the rear ramp of the Bulldog dropped.

Officially named the YS300, the small towing vehicles had long been dubbed "tugboat" by the deck crews in the Confederate Navy because they served the same functions of maneuvering small spacecraft around Cerberus.

"Time to leave, Erin," announced Patterson as he stood and stretched. Johnson likewise stood and stretched as they traded excited looks. Patterson nodded his head and added, "Now it's our turn to bring back exciting discoveries."

Johnson grinned and motioned for Patterson to proceed ahead of her down the ramp. "Age before beauty, Hal."

The two walked down the Bulldog's rear ramp and stopped in surprise. Waiting for them at the bottom of the ramp was Gunnery Sgt. Toshi Kanagawa and four Marines from Echo team. They weren't wearing exosuits, but each of them was armed with a mag-rail rifle.

"Gunny? What's going on?" asked Johnson in a confused voice as Kanagawa saluted.

"Pilot Officer Johnson. Chief Patterson. Please follow me. Do not speak while we are en route to the main conference room."

Patterson and Johnson exchanged confused and concerned looks, then Johnson turned her attention back to Kanagawa.

"Lead the way, Gunny," she said.

Kanagawa nodded towards his four Marines who took up positions surrounding Patterson and Johnson, and the group followed Kanagawa out of the landing bay as the ramp on Bulldog 1 was raised by the deck crew that was getting it ready to move to the hanger.

Confused looks greeted the armed party as they traversed through the corridors of Cerberus. No one spoke, and no one tried to speak to them. It was obvious the group wasn't in a conversational mood.

Within minutes, they arrived at the main conference room and Kanagawa knocked on the metal hatch.

"Enter," came the voice of Lieutenant Gustav.

Kanagawa swung the metal hatch open and walked in. Patterson and Johnson followed him inside, while the four Marines turned and left.

Kanagawa spoke as they walked in. "Patterson and Johnson, reporting in as ordered, sirs."

"Thank you, Gunny. Return to your post," Gustav responded. He was seated at the table with Ronin and Mueller.

Ronin motioned to some open seats. "Grab a seat. You're making me tired just looking at you."

"Yes sir," said Patterson and Johnson simultaneously.

Ronin brought them up to speed. "First of all, whatever you found, we surmise it must be big because the AI suddenly announced your return triggered an automatic security protocol on the ship. Secondly, that's why the Marines escorted you directly here."

Patterson could barely contain his excitement. "Yessir!" he said, drawing the words into one like most of the crew normally did. "We're pretty sure we found something of interest."

Ronin nodded, and continued with a very serious face. "Before you get started, one more thing. This protocol carries a secrecy level that is beyond Top Secret. Breathe a word of it to anyone, so much as drop a hint, and the mandatory penalty is death. There is no appeal, and sentence is required to be carried out immediately."

The surprised look on Gustav's face set a record for raised eyebrows. He knew better than to interrupt a stern lecture like this one. *What kind of secret protocol carries a mandatory death penalty?* he thought to himself. *This must be some hot information.*

Stunned, Johnson and Patterson shared a concerned glance. This wasn't what they had pictured as they returned to Cerberus.

"Yessir. I understand," stammered Johnson. All eyes turned Patterson.

"I understand as well," Patterson stated. He was pretty sure this was being recorded.

"OK. Now that the ground rules have been explained and acknowledged, let's have it," Mueller said, speaking for the first time since their arrival.

Patterson cleared his throat. "Yessir. This is a BLUF report."

Everyone in the room knew BLUF stood for Bottom Line Up Front. Since they arrived under the auspices of the Hades Ordinance, Ronin, Mueller and Gustav were already expecting a BLUF report from the crew of Bulldog 1.

Patterson reached over to the controls to light up the holo unit on the table. "We were proceeding with the mission when we experienced what we initially believed was a mis-jump. Our Bulldog appeared off course and short of our jump coordinates."

The projection by the holo unit changed.

"Instead, we found ourselves 500,000 miles from a giant object located somewhat beyond the edge of the Alioth system."

The image of the dark ring expanded rapidly.

"Once we determined the unidentified object did not appear to present a threat, we investigated further by closing to within visual range. There was no discernible reaction."

Again, the holo replay changed, this time clearly showing the large object.

"As you can see, we found a large ring with a gap measuring approximately 100 miles in diameter. Precise composition of the object is undetermined because our materials scanning failed to identify any alloys or metals that it recognized. Thickness of the ring was uniformly 1 mile. Our inspection revealed a surface that appeared not to contain any features at all. No power signature was noted, and nothing showed up in any scan spectrum to show that the object has a function or is operational."

Patterson cleared his throat slightly before continuing. "We concluded there is a possibility this is a jump gate."

Ronin, Mueller and Gustav all traded quick looks before Ronin spoke. "Aside from fitting our imagining of what one might look like, what makes you think that, Chief?"

In response, Patterson brought up a tactical schematic on the holo before continuing. "Our investigation revealed there seems to be some sort of navigational funnel effect that brings nearby ships which are FTL jumping to the same point. That point is 500,000 miles in front of the ring. Arrival is perfectly aligned with the center of the ring, each time. The funnel extends out at 45 degree angles from the ring for a set distance away from the ring."

As he said this, the lines representing the shape of the funnel appeared on the tactical schematic.

Mueller looked at Patterson. "Any idea how that kept happening, Chief?"

Patterson shook his head. "We don't know how. We just know it was consistent, and we had begun establishing the parameters of the effect. Our scans did not show any measurable power or activity. The region between the ring and the system was filled with highly radioactive debris consisting of dust and rocks of varying size. It was basically a radiation hot spot that fuzzed our sensors if we tried to scan through it."

That was highly unusual. And Ronin only knew of one other radioactive hot spot. The one shielding Planet Nine and Ninebase from the rest of Sol system.

After sharing glances with the others at the table, Ronin decided to ask the ship's artificial intelligence for its thoughts. "AI, do you have sufficient information from the scans that Bulldog 1 brought back to run a comparison with the scans from the hot spot near Ninebase?"

Mueller's eyebrow shot up at that question as the AI responded.

"Processing." Several seconds passed while the AI crunched the data. Just as Ronin was about to speak again, the AI began to convey its results. "Captain, I have compared the data. The radioactive decay evident in the scans suggests there was a large-scale, thermonuclear event in the region between 740 and 775 years ago, which matches the timeline for the creation of the hot spot near Ninebase.

"Isotopic analysis also reveals a match in the isotopes used for the thermonuclear events in both locations. There also appears to be a surprising match in the composition of some of the dust and rocks in both locations."

Gustav tilted his head. "Rocks and dust? What do you mean?" While the match in isotopes wasn't quite as surprising if the ancient nukes came from the same source, there would have been no reason to move rocks from one location to another.

The AI seemed prepared for the question as if it realized it hadn't been totally clear the first time. "A portion of the rocks and dust near the hot spot by Ninebase did not appear to have originated in that solar system, but they align with what our Bulldog teams have found in Alioth system. The converse is also true. Some of the rocks and dust scanned by Bulldog 1 near the Alioth system hot spot appears to originate in other systems, including Earth's system."

Ronin shot a glance at Mueller. "Now THAT is a solid clue that we may have found a gate. AI, any other thoughts on what this is?"

"Captain, while there is insufficient data to confirm the operating hypothesis that this is a jump gate, I nonetheless tentatively tend to agree it is likely was a jump gate. It matches the recent speculation among the fleet's AIs that the technology for jump drives may have been originally intended for short-range travel in a star system."

Now it was Mueller's turn to look confused. "Short-range travel? Why do you say that?"

"The majority opinion among the AIs is that the jump drives were primarily intended to get ships to the jump gates, which themselves were the primary method of travel between star systems with corresponding gates. And that it was the secondary purpose of jump drives to enable exploration missions to systems that lacked a gate. Due to the greater risks associated with navigational error and unknown navigational hazards when jumping to new destinations, the AI majority opinion is that the jump gates likely provided a faster and safer method of travel. That would have meant the jump gates were the preferred and primary option, if a gate were available."

After the unusually long report from his famously terse AI, Ronin leaned back his seat and blew out a small sigh. Everyone just looked at him.

Breaking the moment of silence that followed, Ronin announced his decision. "We need more information. A lot more. About the possible civilization in the Alioth system. And about the possible jump gate outside the system."

His eyes fell upon Johnson and Patterson, who both appeared surprised at his statement about a possible civilization. They'd been so busy with the ring, they hadn't been aware of what other information the remaining Bulldogs had returned with. "I know Lieutenant Sunderland isn't here, but how difficult do you think it would be to seed the area with sensor and observation drones?"

Johnson shrugged her shoulders. "Not very, Captain. They'll have to be heavily shielded to protect them from all that radiation in the region, but the deployment won't take more than a couple of days. Less, if we are joined by other Bulldog crews."

Ronin nodded and thumbed open a commlink. "Lieutenant Sunderland, this is the Captain."

Sunderland's voice floated over the commlink. "Aye, sir, who do you want us to shoot down?"

Ronin snorted. "Nothing fun like that on today's agenda, Lieutenant. We're going to transmit some data to you. Use it to design a drone surveillance net with high resolution optics and our best sensor packages. As soon as you're ready, expect to deploy it immediately using Bulldogs 1 and 2."

"Yessir, I'll get right on it," Sunderland confirmed.

"Lieutenant, the data and mission are classified above top secret," Ronin added.

Sunderland's surprise was evident in the tone of his voice more so than his words. "Really? We'll act accordingly, sir. I'll read in the crew of Bulldog 2 on the secrecy level."

"Excellent. Ronin out." With that, Ronin cut the commlink to Sunderland. His eyes flicked back to Johnson and Patterson. "I'm sending you both back for the seeding of the drone net as you're already familiar with the situation. Go hit the showers and grab some chow. Get some rack time if possible."

Both heads nodded in unison, and Patterson and Johnson simultaneously replied, "Yessir." Trading glances, they stood and departed the main conference room. After they closed the hatch behind them, Mueller spoke.

"Keeping the science teams aboard for now?" she asked.

Ronin nodded. "Yep. Drone surveillance can capture and relay all the data to the teams on Cerberus for now. I'm hedging our bets against the possibility we might need our teams on the ship when we get further down into the system."

Everyone present knew that moving "down" into a star system simply meant getting closer to the star.

Gustav nodded. He had been studying the AI's summary of the information that the other Bulldogs had brought back with them. "Yessir," he said. "We've detected significant levels of encrypted comms traffic emanating from somewhere in that system. They're using multiple bandwidths, and our AI has opined they are using more than one type of encryption."

Mueller added her observation of that data. "There seems to be a correlation between certain types of encryption being used only in conjunction with comms traffic on particular bandwidths."

Gustav and Ronin both looked thoughtful. "Kind of like there being comms traffic from differing entities," Ronin said quietly.

Gustav's attention was drawn to Ronin when he said that. "You think there isn't a unified government in this system?"

Ronin had definitely thought of that. "Possibly. The level of comms traffic matches the volumes we would expect from a planet with a population on it instead of bases or just a bunch of ships and naval activity, so that makes me suspect it's a planet. I also doubt it's more than one planet, because the amount of comms traffic doesn't seem high enough for two."

The quiet of the next few moments was broken by Gustav. "I hope they treat visitors more hospitably than Terra Station's government did."

Ronin and Mueller nodded. "Agreed," they said in unison.

CHAPTER 13

FINAL APPROACH

"We're jumping Cerberus into the system's asteroid field?" asked Lieutenant LeCroy, who was sitting at the tactical station with Commander Mueller.

Mueller nodded. "That's affirmative. Based on the scouting of our Bulldog teams, there are multiple facilities operating in the belt, and there are vast areas which are unoccupied."

She pointed to the tactical map being displayed on LeCroy's screen. "This point in the unoccupied zone of the belt is Dixie Station for this mission," she noted.

LeCroy nodded now, too. "OK. Tacnet has been updated with Dixie Station designated for those coordinates."

He expanded another part of the tactical map of the belt. "These are the facilities we've found. This group I've marked in purple all appear to be automated mining operations. The group in yellow are mining operations that seem to have intermittent visitation from crewed ships."

LeCroy paused to draw a breath and highlighted another group of coordinates on the screen by pressing a button. "The data for this group in green suggests these operations have permanent crews, but there is too much dust and rocks in the region for our scanners to confirm. That also means we can't be sure what else is there, including military installations."

Mueller nodded. It was as she expected. "We're not fans of jumping in blindly either, but we think that may be a lower risk encounter than jumping deeper into the system and possibly causing a hostile response. Or one that's on a larger scale."

LeCroy looked at her. "I'd like to avoid that this go round. It wasn't a good feeling to bomb parts of Terra Station back to the Stone Age because they attacked Cerberus when we arrived in orbit," he said, reaching over to activate another group of coordinates on his screen.

"Last group is in red. We have reason to believe these are military assets and installations. We'll avoid those unless we have a good reason to visit."

Mueller's face scrunched up slightly. "Did you notice in the data that those military installations don't all operate using the same technology and standards?" she asked as Ronin joined them at the tactical station.

Ronin answered Mueller's question. "Based on the observed technologies, encryption schemes and design standards, we've identified what I believe are seven distinctly different military Factions."

LeCroy's eyes grew wide. Delacroix turned his head to look over at them with a concerned look when he overheard that statement from his scanning station.

"Seven? Do we know if they're rival Factions, or are there alignments of Factions?" LeCroy asked.

Ronin shook his head. "We got nothing regarding that. Comm traffic out here is all encrypted. I've ordered a scouting mission deeper into the system that departs from Cerberus once we arrive at Dixie Station, but so far we have detected no unencrypted communications that we can read. Right now, we're left guessing."

Ronin looked at LeCroy's screen and pointed with his chin to the tactical map on Tacnet that was on it. "Lieutenant, let's identify several suitable installations we can pay a visit to. One that's distant from any probable military installations. We'll supplement those recommendations with any intel the scouts bring back from further down the system."

"Very good, sir. I'll send you my recommendations as soon as they're ready."

CHAPTER 14

WARSPITE

"We will hit the Cosa Nostra at Il Mio Dieci," said Lars Berven in his deep and gravelly voice. As captain of the Ullr longship Warspite, Berven commanded the attention of his warriors. Right now, his top warriors were gathered around him in the galley of Warspite.

Carrying a crew of 100, the Warspite featured four drive engines at the aft end of an elongated, mostly smooth cigar-shaped hull. The vessel carried multiple missile launchers and a few small railguns for close-in work. The few protrusions from the hull were exterior mounts, which the Ullr called "racks," to attach pods and small manned boarding craft.

As Berven glared around, he saw heads with grim expressions begin to nod. "We will have our revenge for their Raider's attack on our mine, and for their destruction of Captain Olsen's longship."

The warriors suddenly roared their approval, many holding their weapons aloft as they did so, as if they getting themselves pumped up for battle. Battleaxes, various knives, rifles, and some pistols were soon waiving around in the thunderous cheering. Berven know the sound traveled down the cramped halls of the longship, and he approved.

Berven motioned to quiet them down so he could continue. "Il Mio Dieci is Asteroid Mine Number 10 to them, and it has a significant civilian population present. Destroy their defenses, and we will conquer them."

"We will take their women!" shouted one of the warriors.

Berven again motioned for them to quiet down. "We WILL take their women, yes. And their gold. And their jewels. And anything else we can grab!"

The cheering drowned out Berven's next words, so he quieted them one more time. "Return to your stations, brothers. And we will make the gods proud when we strike!"

This time the roar of the warriors could be heard everywhere on the Warspite.

CHAPTER 15

OPERATIONS

"**O**ur target is a civilian mining installation on this asteroid," LeCroy said as he pressed a button to highlight on the holo projected above the table the particular rock in the asteroid belt he was talking about.

Gustav's eyes glanced around the officers and marine gunnery sergeants assembled in the main conference room to get a read on what they were thinking. As he did so, Echo team leader, Gunnery Sergeant Blackwater, tilted his head slightly to the side as he asked a question. "Lieutenant, how close are the known military assets to this installation?"

LeCroy responded immediately. "Based on the lack of detected activity beyond the belt, our operating assumption is whoever occupies this system lacks an FTL drive. We had to draw upon known sublight speeds from our pre-jump drive days to arrive at an estimate. Factoring that in, this installation is a week's travel from the nearest known military asset."

Without FTL, everyone knew it would be terribly impracticable to have operations further up the system due to the sheer distance. The officers and Marines stirred uncomfortably at LeCroy's words.

There isn't much beyond the belt anyway, so a lack of FTL capability isn't surprising, thought Delacroix. *One dwarf planet, with an even smaller moon. At least there are three planets inside the belt's ring around the sun.* Delacroix remained silent and refocused on LeCroy's briefing.

"That's an awful lot of unknowns and guessing, Lieutenant," remarked Sunderland. As the ship's CAG (Commander, Air-Group), he was expected to be present as well.

LeCroy nodded in agreement. "Yes, it is. The number of known-unknowns carries a lot of risk for this operation. Not to mention the number of unknown-unknowns." LeCroy couldn't say much else except to acknowledge the obvious. Captain Ronin saved him.

"We all know the risks here. Space is an unforgiving place, and exploring it is a high-risk proposition. We'll minimize risks when we can, but for this op, we'll repeat the first contact protocol from Terra Station by seeding a drone screen in the airspace near the rock, and then sending in a Bulldog with an ambassador.

"We'll be working with less intel than on the Terra Station mission, though, because we already know all the comms traffic is encrypted. Dr. Mueller's team is working on cracking the codes, but he has said not to expect any success in the near future as their encryption is far advanced compared to Terra Station's."

Heads around the room nodded. This was an experienced crew, and they knew better than to expect total safety. Definitely not out in deep space, and especially not when exploring other star systems.

"OK. Any questions?" Ronin said as he looked at each of them. "Alright. Don't hesitate to ask if one comes up in your pre-ops planning. Report readiness status by 0900 tomorrow and we'll push off 12 hours after that. For this op, we'll position Cerberus a short jump from the objective in case things go sideways and the Bulldog needs backup. Dismissed."

Everyone filed out, leaving Commander Mueller and Ronin alone in the conference room. They looked at each other for a moment, then Mueller spoke."The ship's image projection capability will be severely compromised out here in the belt."

Ronin nodded. "I know. And we can't just jump back and forth between Dixie Station and the objective. There's just too much interference from all the rocks and dust for long range navigation."

Mueller nodded now. "Best we can do is pick a good hide nearby, and hope nothing stumbles across us."

"Exactly." Ronin smiled. She totally got it.

CHAPTER 16

KNOCK KNOCK

"Course for the mining facility laid in, Captain. Per your orders, we are jumping in a wide azimuth to the center of the system and taking a different approach into the objective," announced Lt. Antonio Perez from the ship's helm, as he turned slightly and looked over at Ronin and Mueller.

Ronin and Mueller were both standing next to the captain's chair in the dimmed lights of the Bridge. After nodding a response to Perez, Mueller glanced at Ronin and whispered very quietly, "The extra jump is taking us wide of the funnel effect of the ring that Bulldog 1 located?"

Ronin nodded slightly and spoke equally as softly. "Yeah. We now know the size of the ring's funnel effect thanks to the drones and scouting by the Bulldogs, and there's little sense in risking the ship by jumping too close to it."

Mueller looked thoughtful for a moment. "Good. It'd be better if a fully equipped scientific research ship investigated rather than a warship like Cerberus.

"Captain? The ship is ready to jump," Perez said, both as a question and as a subtle reminder they're waiting to get started.

Ronin half-smiled, and sat in the captain's chair. His face turned serious. "Lt. Perez, execute the series of jumps," he ordered.

Smiling now, Perez turned back to his board as he replied, "Aye, aye, sir. Executing jump 1 in 5, 4, 3, 2, 1. Jumping."

Cerberus disappeared, and reappeared along the rim of the system with a tiny jump flare. Seconds later, the ship jumped again. The process repeated a few times until they arrived at the coordinates designated as their planned operations area.

"We've arrived at our hide near the mining facility, Captain."

"Very well," Ronin said, then he thumbed open a commlink.

"Sunderland here, Captain," answered the ship's air group commander.

"CAG, launch Bulldog 7," ordered Ronin.

"Launching now, Captain," came Sunderland's crisp reply. He ended the commlink and opened another to Bulldog 7, which was sitting in the launch bay.

"Bulldog 7, you are a go for launch," Sunderland said.

"Roger that. Launching," responded Pilot Officer Greg Lowridge, who was strapped into the pilot's seat of Bulldog 7. Lowridge and his rearseater, Chief Paul Drayson, were relative newcomers to the Cerberus flight crews. They had replaced Bulldog 4 after it had been destroyed during the Battle of the Dark Side during the war against the Collective. The assault shuttle shot out of the launch tube. It jumped away soon after leaving Cerberus.

"Bulldog 7 has jumped away, Captain," reported Delacroix from his scanning station.

Ronin nodded slightly to Delacroix in response. "Now we wait."

CHAPTER 17

BULLDOG 7

"Distance to the mining installation ... 650,000 miles. No spacecraft in the area. No threats detected. We're right where we're supposed to be," noted Drayson in a distracted tone of voice. He was in his usual spot as the rearseater for Bulldog 7 and was closely monitoring his scanners.

Lowridge glanced back at him from the pilot's seat in the cockpit. "You expected something else?" he said teasingly as he traded glances with their passenger, Dr. Winston Wright.

Drayson snorted. "Stop it, or I'm opening the can of smoked oysters I smuggled on board."

"No!" roared Lowridge in tone of faked despair.

"Wait, you have smoked oysters?" Wright asked, suddenly becoming highly interested.

"You a smoked oysters man, Doc?" Drayson asked.

"Oh, yeah!" Wright said enthusiastically. "It's a weakness of mine."

"Doc, I don't care what they say about you, if you're a smoked oysters man, you're alright in my book," Drayson responded wryly. "They're in my go-bag over there in the utility compartment to your left," said Drayson, waving vaguely in the direction over his right shoulder. His eyes remained glued to his screens.

"ETA to target, 3 hours 23 minutes at current speed and course," Drayson announced, interrupting the oysters discussion while Wright foraged in the utility compartment for the hidden go-bag.

"Ugh. It's going to stink in here for hours! You are a bad, bad man," Lowridge complained loudly.

"I resent that. Ain't it great?" smirked Drayson.

"Who wants some?" Wright called as he came back forward with the can of oysters and some plates with crackers. He didn't seem surprised when both Drayson and Lowridge reached behind themselves with open hands.

***

"Distance to the mining installation, 75,000 miles and closing rapidly," announced Drayson. "No contacts yet, but they've created so much dust that it's really interfering with our scans," he added.

Lowridge grunted an acknowledgment as he began chewing on his third piece of oyster. The cabin smelled like oysters, and he was getting restless.

From all the way to the back of the shuttle, Lowridge could hear soft snoring from Dr. Wright, which didn't help his mood. *When it comes to grabbing some shut-eye when you can, for once Wright isn't wrong*, he thought irritably. A nap sounded pretty good about now.

A few more minutes passed in silence that was only broken by Wright's snores and the ambient noise of the shuttle, until the sound of a warning alarm poured out of Drayson's station.

"Contact! We're being pinged by a scan. Attempting to identify direction and distance," Drayson said loudly.

"Affirmative. I've spun up the jump drives for emergency jump if need be," Lowridge responded without turning around. His boredom evaporated the instant the warning alarm sounded.

By now, the commotion had awakened Dr. Wright. He moved forward and stood behind Drayson, looking at the rearseater's screen in silence. Even Wright knew not to interrupt them.

"AI confirms this is no navigational beacon. Range to bogey ... 11,000 miles to starboard and closing rapidly. Down angle is 15 degrees," Drayson reported rapidly as the unidentified vessel was approaching from below and to their right.

Seconds ticked by until Drayson spoke again. "Whoever they are, their ship is still accelerating like a fat kid skiing down a cliff. It's almost like a ship-to-ship missile, but the profile doesn't match one. Range now 8,000 miles and closing."

Lowridge's finger hovered near the blinking button on his station that would jump the shuttle away. "Have they acquired weapons lock?" he asked.

Drayson shook his head, even though neither of them was looking at one another. "No. There's too much interference out there. I'm going to squawk the FFI and see if they react to it."

Drayson didn't explain to Dr. Wright that FFI was the Friend or Foe Identification of a Confederate Navy vessel. Drayson activated the FFI.

It didn't take long for Drayson to detect a change. "We're receiving an encrypted auto-reply. We can't read it!" he shouted.

With a concerned look on his face, Lowridge glanced at Dr. Wright. "Doc, I think you better go get your exosuit on. If this goes sideways, you won't have enough time to do it then."

With an expression that was half-fear and half-surprise, Wright nodded and left to get geared up.

CHAPTER 18

WARSPITE

"**M**aking our final turn for Il Mio Dieci in two minutes, Captain," reported the helmsman.

"Any signs they've detected us?" asked Berven, his piercing blue eyes blazing in the dim of the Warspite's bridge. He had dressed in his usual uniform for the attack—weathered, dark brown leather armor, boots, and an assortment of knives strapped to his torso. Berven's head was bald and scarred, and his heavy beard was salted with grey in it. He screwed his face into a visage of concentration as they approached the target. Protective leather hid battle scars on his arms and torso. On his back, he bore the healed scars from the swipe of a Hellcat. Its long fanged teeth now dangled from the chain around his neck.

"Negative. They're just civilians. They're still not vigilant enough against possible hostiles," reported the warrior manning the ship's weapons station.

Berven drummed his fingers impatiently, willing his ship to stay hidden long enough to initiate their attack once they closed the remaining distance. They were still tens of thousands of miles away from the target.

A warning alarm began beeping at the weapons station, and the warrior manning the station suddenly announced. "Proximity alarm! Unidentified vessel, inbound towards the target. Configuration ... unknown. Hull type ... unknown. Propulsion type ... unknown. Weapons ... also unknown." A few more seconds elapsed while he collected additional data.

Recognizing that being discovered at this stage of their approach jeopardized their mission, Berven immediately shouted, "Course change.

Intercept that vessel. Prepare for immediate combat." He didn't bother to order the crew to their battle stations because they already occupied those in anticipation of their assault on Il Mio Dieci.

Berven took a couple seconds to walk to the weapons station. He remained quiet, his attention on his warrior. The warrior was competent, and Berven knew not to interrupt him without good reason.

"Vessel size is equivalent to a large shuttle, or a small cargo hauler. Speed is high. Distance 8,000 and closing rapidly. We're receiving some kind of signal from them. It says they're a Confederate Navy shuttle?" the warrior stated, making the final sentence a question.

His face adopting a confused expression, Berven suddenly exclaimed, "Confederate Navy? What Confederacy?" He cast a look about the bridge at the other warriors and then asked, "Any of you ever heard of a Confederacy somewhere?"

Heads shook in response.

"It's got to be some kind of trick. Open a channel and ask this Navy," Berven said, calling over to his warrior at the communications station, snidely emphasizing the word Navy, "if they have an emissary on board and if we can come along side."

"We're talking?" asked the communications warrior in surprise. All the heads on the bridge turned towards Berven. Surprise and shock was on all their faces. Ullrians didn't negotiate with anybody. They also weren't known for taking prisoners of combatants either.

In response, Berven glared back at them. "We're using it as a ruse to get close. I want weapons manned and ready, when we get close enough we'll take them out and continue on to Il Mio Dieci.

Evil grins spread across the warriors' faces. Subterfuge was going to be icing on the cake.

"They've accepted the 'request,' Captain," said the communications officer a few minutes later.

"Bring us alongside. Use passive tracking to lock the ship's weapons on the target. I don't want them getting spooked," Berven said as he returned to his chair.

His craggy face and voice were deadly serious now. "Soon, my friends. Soon. You will be sent to meet your gods," he whispered to himself.

CHAPTER 19

BULLDOG 7

"**P**aul, what can you tell us about them?" asked Dr. Wright. Surprised at the use of his first name, Drayson glanced up at Wright, who was now in his exosuit and standing next to Drayson's station.

He shook his head. "Not a lot. It's a long, elongated hull with few protrusions, and exterior racks for attachments. Some of those attachments might be smaller ships. Length is about 500 feet, so it's only as long as Cerberus is wide. Looks like four fusion drive engines, but they're of incredible power and efficiency. Almost off the charts engine power in fact. Hull composition appears to be of unknown alloyed armor. Beyond that, we don't have much as our scans aren't penetrating their hull."

Dr. Wright tilted his head to the side. "Not much to go on, is it?"

Drayson half smiled as he continued scanning. "Nope. Welcome to space, Doc. By the way, they'll be here in a few minutes. Time to fully button up our exosuits and we'll go on commlinks from here on out." Each of them quickly finished doing so and the suits linked together on a common commlink that Drayson opened.

Wright settled into his seat on the shuttle. He could feel beads of sweat forming on his brow. Not because the exosuit was too warm. His nerves were causing it.

The minutes passed quickly. "Arrival time, two minutes," Drayson said, breaking the tense silence. "Their speed is slowing and they are coming about. They actually are maneuvering to come alongside!" he said, relief evident in his voice. "They're well within voice range. Receiving incoming signal," Drayson added as he piped the message directly into the commlink for all of them.

A gravelly voice filled their ears.

"Unidentified vessel, this is the Longship Warspite. We are pulling alongside as agreed. Can you identify for us what Confederation you hail from? We are not familiar with it."

Eyebrows raised inside his exosuit, Lowridge checked to make sure they weren't on an open line to Warspite before speaking on the open commlink to Wright and Drayson. "Doc, I think you're up on this one."

Nodding Wright responded to the other ship's query. "Warspite, this is Dr. Winston Wright. I am the Confederate representative from Earth."

CHAPTER 20

WARSPITE

"**W**arspite, this is Dr. Winston Wright. I am the Confederate representative from Earth," came the strangely accented voice over the channel. The warriors on the bridge traded confused looks. The target lock lights at the weapons station being crewed by the Ullrian warrior began turning green, and he offered a silent thumbs up to a watchful Berven when they all completed their targeting.

Smiling without mirth, Berven nodded to the weapons officer and raised his hand in a "wait for my signal" motion. Unable to help himself, Berven broke out into laughter, unconcerned with the possibility of being heard over the channel by the unidentified ship.

"Earth! Earth is just a myth like any other legend," Berven replied, as he watched the screen where their distance from the other ship was being measured. It was still falling rapidly. "There are plenty of lost civilization myths like Earth and Atlantis or Forrestal and Celestra." As he said this, his eyes grew wide as the number steadied, indicating their relative distance had stabilized. Berven dropped his arm and pointed at the weapons station.

Warspite juddered with weapons release.

***

Wright was about to respond when an alarm suddenly sounded from Drayson's station.

"Weapons launch!" yelled Drayson.

Having been lulled into a false sense of security, Lowridge's finger stabbed down towards the button to jump the ship from where it had been resting on the shuttle's flight stick.

Before Lowridge's finger completed the panicked motion, the shuttle was torn apart by the point-blank missile impact that erased the front half of Bulldog 7 in a kinetic explosion. There was a brief fire from the sudden mix of sparks, oxygen, and fuel, which the vacuum of space snuffed out in seconds.

On the Warspite's bridge, Berven stared intently at one of the view screens near his workstation. His concentration was interrupted when the warrior manning the weapons station spoke.

"Direct hit, Captain. The front half of the vessel has been destroyed and we're reading no power levels on the remainder. Do you wish to claim the rest as salvage?"

Looking over at the weapons station, Berven glared and shook his head. He wasn't angry with the warrior; it was Berven's blood lust at killing whoever was unfortunate enough to be in that ship. "Negative. We proceed with our mission to Il Mio Dieci. This little shuttle isn't worth our trouble. We just had to take them out of the game before they could raise an alarm."

CHAPTER 21

DR. WINSTON WRIGHT

"Wake up, Dr. Wright. Wake up, Dr. Wright. Wake up, Dr. Wright. Wake ..."

"I'm awake, please stop!" Wright said slowly as he regained consciousness. He gasped for air and opened his eyes. Stars spun crazily in his vision.

It took a few moments for Wright to understand what he was seeing. The stars weren't tumbling around—he was the one doing the tumbling.

"Computer, stabilize my orientation," Wright ordered after a few moments.

"Acknowledged. Please be advised, most of your exosuit's maneuvering jets are offline. It will take longer to stop your tumble."

Wright nodded to himself. "Understood. Please proceed, and provide a status report."

He felt his suit start to emit small bursts of thrust and could see his tumble begin to slow as his exosuit spoke to him.

"You lost consciousness for five minutes. Your exosuit is heavily damaged and losing life support due to the reduced integrity. You have 10 percent of your remaining maneuvering jets, although fuel levels are not critical. Breathable atmosphere is depleted in two hours, ten minutes. Heat is depleted in 1 hour, 35 minutes. External commlink system is inoperational. External sensors, fully functional. On-board computer, fully functional. The main wreckage of Bulldog 7 is 300 yards distant. Emergency auto-distress beacon was deployed and is operational at last contact. Pilot Officer Greg Lowridge is deceased. Current status of Chief Paul Drayson is unknown as his suit telemetry is offline."

As the exosuit's computer system reported all this to Wright, it continued to deftly micro-burst its jets to bring Wright's tumble under control.

Two hours! And I'll freeze to death out here before I run out of air, Wright thought sourly. *Maybe now's a good time to reevaluate my excitement about today's mission,* he said to himself.

Wright held himself very still for a few minutes, letting his exosuit do all the work to stop the tumble while he mulled over the computer's report. Something didn't make sense.

"Computer, what does the auto-distress beacon do?" Wright asked suddenly.

"The auto-distress beacon deploys when a ship suffers catastrophic damage. It broadcasts a signal to all Confederation ships in the area about the incident."

Wright looked perplexed for a moment inside his exosuit. "Computer, approximately how long will it take the distress signal to reach Cerberus at its last known location?"

"Six hours, 46 minutes at sublight speeds."

Wright sighed in spite of himself. *Fat lot of good that will do,* he thought. "What did you mean when you said 'at last contact' when you reported on the beacon deployment?" Wright said, grasping at any small hope.

"Bulldog 7 was equipped with the upgraded auto-distress beacon system that is jump drive enabled. The beacon jumped to the rendezvous point soon after it deployed." As the computer finished saying this, it gave the exosuit one final jolt to stop its tumbling. Wright looked around now and spotted the wreckage of the Bulldog. It was highlighted on his visor by the computer because he would have had a difficult time locating it with the naked eye in space at this distance.

"Computer, navigate us to the remains of Bulldog 7," Wright ordered. His suit jets began the process of safely moving him through the debris field to close with the back half of Bulldog 7. Even though it was only about 300 yards, it consumed both precious time and fuel to reach it.

As he approached Bulldog 7, Wright noted it didn't have much tumble or spin to it. *Of course, I'm much smaller and had been ejected from the shuttle, which might account for the difference*, he thought to himself as he reached out to grasp a ragged edge of the hull to slow his momentum. Turning on his exterior lights, Wright peered around the edge into the shuttle.

"Drayson!" he exclaimed in surprise. Chief Drayson was still belted into his seat, and his back was to Wright.

Noticing Drayson wasn't moving, Wright carefully pulled himself over to Drayson. He managed to avoid tearing his exosuit on any sharp edges or debris floating inside the dark interior.

Wright reached out to tap Drayson on shoulder to get his attention. The gentle motion caused Drayson to slump forward, so Wright pulled himself to the front so he could get a better look at him. Drayson was dead. His helmet visor had been punctured by shrapnel and Wright could see it was covered in blood from the inside.

"Dr. Wright, the exosuit sensors have detected a ship approaching."

"Identify!" Wright ordered fearfully. He tore his eyes away from Drayson's corpse and glanced out through where the front of the shuttle once was.

"Confederate Navy class Bulldog. This exosuit's external commlink system is still inoperable. Do you wish to communicate by signal light?" the computer replied.

"We can do that? Yes, tell them there is only one survivor, we have two KIA with one missing, and we need a lift as my exosuit is damaged and losing life support." Wright said as he moved to the edge of the shuttle to make himself more visible.

Within seconds, his suit began transmitting the message by blinking its exterior lights. The light on the arriving Bulldog flashed twice as it came to a relative stop with the wreckage. "We have received confirmation of message receipt by the Bulldog," said the exosuit's computer to Wright.

Wright sighed with the wave of relief that washed over him. On the side of his rescue shuttle was a large number 3, signifying the arrival of Pilot Officer Antonio Russo and his rearseater, Chief Michael Jonsey.

CHAPTER 22

CERBERUS

"The sensor drone net and commlink relays we deployed are functioning within normal parameters, Captain. They'll relay an alert over to Cerberus at our current location if anything arrives at the rendezvous point," Delacroix stated. He was standing with Mueller and Ronin at the sensor station on the Bridge.

Mueller nodded. "Bulldog 7 should reach the mining installation in a little over two hours. Fingers crossed this doesn't play out like our arrival at Terra Station," she said to the two of them.

As she said it, Ronin's eyes flicked to the mission timer in the corner of the screen at the scanning station. He nodded as he noted how many hours the shuttle had been away from Cerberus. "Yes. Anything but th–" he began saying when LeCroy suddenly interrupted them from the tactical station.

"Contact! The drone net just relayed a report that Bulldog 7's emergency auto-distress beacon jumped into the rendezvous point and the shuttle has been destroyed by an unidentified ship."

Ronin responded quickly and loudly by ordering, "Action stations!"

While the ship's klaxon sounded, he and Mueller swiftly moved to their seats at the center of the Bridge.

LeCroy put an image of an unfamiliar ship on the main view screen. "Captain, all combat stations report manned and ready. This image was relayed from the auto-distress beacon. It's the ship that attacked Bulldog 7."

Delacroix spoke immediately after LeCroy. "Captain, scans show no ships or identified threats. The drone net is likewise reporting the same for the auto-distress beacon over at the rendezvous point."

Perez nearly interrupted Delacroix. "Jump drive is spun up and coordinates entered into the navigation computer to execute an emergency jump, Captain."

Mueller nodded and looked at LeCroy. "Lieutenant, what do we know about that ship?" she asked.

"Bulldog 7 was only able to collect superficial information as the unknown alloy used in the ship's hull composition deflected most attempts to scan and fully profile the vessel. It has four fusion drive engines. Video replay of the attack shows multiple missile launchers and a few small railguns."

As LeCroy spoke, he cast different pictures over to the main view screen that now contained images of what he was talking about. "It has a long, elongated hull with few protrusions and some exterior attachment racks. Some of the attachments appear to include these small manned craft you see in this picture."

LeCroy paused to take a breath before continuing. "Length is about 500 feet, so it's only as long as Cerberus is wide. Sensors indicate the fusion drive engines have incredible power and efficiency. Almost off the charts engine power in fact, so in a sublight race, this vessel can outrun and out accelerate anything in the Confederate Navy."

"How much acceleration are we talking about?" Ronin asked.

LeCroy looked at Ronin as he spoke. "About 25 gravities, Captain. Which means their internal gravity dampeners must be powerful enough to accommodate that much push or the crew wouldn't survive for long. The AI is speculating the hostile lacks FTL drives based on its approach to Bulldog 7. It approached at sublight speeds and the ship used a communications pretext to get within point blank range before firing on our shuttle. They were so close there wasn't time for an emergency jump."

Ronin and Mueller traded surprised looks, each mirroring the raised eyebrow of the other. "Communications?" Mueller said, both as a question and as a statement.

"Yes, Commander, I'll play the time-compressed audio over the Bridge's speakers now," LeCroy said.

Everyone on the Bridge listened intently to the communications between their destroyed shuttle and the hostile vessel. No one spoke until they heard, "There are plenty of lost civilization myths like Earth and Atlantis or Forrestal and Celestra."

LeCroy spoke first. "That was the final communication before the hostile opened fire. Before it jumped away, the beacon's sensors noted the hostile vessel departed for the mining installation that Bulldog 7 was en route to."

By now, most of the Bridge crew was looking at Ronin, who had a look of intense concentration on his face. He thumbed open a commlink. "Lieutenant Sunderland, this is the Captain."

"Yes, Captain?" came Sunderland's immediate reply from the pilot's ready room. The ship's pilots were gathered there, awaiting either a Go order for combat, or a Stand Down order.

"Lieutenant, Bulldog 7 has been attacked and destroyed. Send two Bulldogs to the coordinates where the attack occurred. Equip one for search and rescue, and the other with a weapons pod. Lieutenant LeCroy is sending you tactical information on the vessel that attacked and the coordinates. As soon as your shuttles are away, we're going after the ship that did this," Ronin said, anger plainly evident in his voice.

His voice all business, Sunderland crisply replied, "Right away, Captain. It'll take 15 minutes to get the Bulldogs configured and out the launch tubes. The Tomcat squadrons will be ready to man their fighters as soon as you give the word."

"Thank you, CAG. Ronin out."

Ronin closed the commlink and glanced around at the Bridge crew's faces looking at him. "I'm pretty sure we know exactly where that ship is headed. There's no other reason for it to have gone that direction as there's nothing else there. Perez, prepare to jump Cerberus directly to the mining installation after our shuttles are away."

"Aye, Captain," Perez said as he turned back to his station. He kept his concerns about jumping into a dust and rock filled region of space to himself.

Ronin looked at the tactical and scanning stations. "LeCroy, Delacroix—Cerberus will be coming in hot. Find that ship as soon as we jump in and feed the firing solutions to our weapons systems. Jump bombs are authorized."

A chorus of "yessirs" rose from LeCroy and Delacroix as they prepared to execute Ronin's combat orders.

"You're thinking this hostile also isn't a friendly to the mining installation, aren't you?" Mueller asked quietly.

Ronin nodded to her. "Precisely. By far the most likely tactical scenario for the hostile vessel to initiate a sneak attack to destroy an unknown shuttle like that is as a precaution to keep it from sounding an alarm for the mining installation. The AI believes we are dealing with rival groups based on the data we've found so far. Possibly as many as seven distinctly different groups. If we save one group's facility from an attack by a rival, that might curry us some favor. But there's certainly more than one reason to light up the hostile."

Now it was Mueller's turn to nod. "To teach them a lesson never to attack us."

"Precisely," said Ronin.

CHAPTER 23

BATTLE OF IL MIO DIECI

"**W**hich Faction do you think that shuttle was from? I never heard an accent like that before," rumbled the gravely bass voice of Eric the Dour as he absentmindedly ran a thumb over the point of the battleaxe attached to his hip. He was on the bridge of Warspite, watching the screens that showed their approach to Il Mio Dieci and standing next to his old friend, Berven.

Berven glanced slightly at Eric. They'd been fighting and raiding together for over 20 years. Despite all that time, Eric remained an enigma. Eric was of unknown ancestry and had no known last name. Not one that he had ever shared, anyway.

Eric had ironically been dubbed "the Dour" for his penchant to sing battle songs when his spirits were high, and that only occurred when there was killing or raiding to be done. Nothing else seemed to make him happy. Eric the Dour lived for battle, and he was not one to withhold glorification of a courageous and valiant enemy. He also was not one to withhold contempt for any enemy who refused to fight or who wasn't very good at fighting.

Eric's dirty blonde hair hung in an unkempt fashion from his head, and he paid little heed to how huge he was compared to most other Solarans. He was 6'4" and while that height wasn't terribly unusual on Earth, it certainly was on a heavy gravity world like Solara. Centuries of natural selection from 1.5 gravities had resulted in a shorter, stouter breed of human.

Taller, thinner Solarans tended to die young and without leaving off-spring. Those with shorter, stronger physiques lived longer and passed on their traits that better withstood the gravity. One of the problems when fighting someone like Eric the Dour was not that he was tall—it was that he was still stout and strong. He was a genetic freak who had created as many offspring as possible, so there would be many more like him in the future.

Berven had been musing over the same questions as Eric, and rumbled his own in return. "Strange accent. Unknown, advanced ship type. We weren't hidden from their instrumentation in the slightest. That doesn't match up with any Solaran Faction. We might be looking at a new kind of war."

Eric the Dour snorted. "Challenge accepted. I will enjoy finding new ways to kill them. The only good enemy is a worthy one."

Berven nodded slowly, his eyes now on the screen, which had a countdown timer on it. Just over an hour until they arrived at Il Mio Dieci. "It is time. Gather your warriors and make ready to board the enemy. You'll launch soon."

"With pleasure!" Eric rumbled enthusiastically as he turned to leave. His gravelly bass voice started singing a battle song of conquest and victory as he exited the bridge.

Berven watched Eric as he left. They had been friends a long time, but Berven didn't share the depth of his concern about the shuttle they had destroyed. *Who were they?* He brooded over the question, but more importantly he kept asking himself, *Were there any more of them?*

His eyes moved back to the screen and its countdown timer. Not long now, and they could get on with the raid. The dimly lit bridge was quiet as everyone concentrated on their tasks.

The quiet was soon broken by the sound of an electronic warning alarm. Berven's head whipped around to look at the source, which was the station where the ship's scanning functions were controlled. The warrior operating the station suddenly said, "Proximity alarm! Unknown vessel ahead, it's positioned between Warspite and Il Mio Dieci. Unknown configuration and unknown origin. Size is unlike anything we've ever seen!"

"How large?" Berven asked.

"Over twenty times our size! We're not observing any power readings, but it's clearly maneuvering. Long-range optics have captured an image, I'm putting it on screens now."

Every set of eyes on the bridge tuned into the screens at their stations. The image was, to say the least, alarming. It was a huge vessel that somehow was sleek in appearance despite her size. She had a tapered prow in front and huge drive engines in the rear. From this angle, they could clearly see a landing bay located along her length.

"How come there's no tail from the fusion drives?" asked the warrior at the scanning station. It was essentially a rhetorical question, but Berven had a bad feeling about the answer.

"Who says it uses fusion drives for propulsion?" Berven noted dryly. Every head on the bridge turned to look at him.

Berven decided to elaborate. "We don't know who they are, or what tech they have. And we don't have much time to figure it out."

"Time to intercept ... 20 minutes, Captain," suddenly reported the warrior operating the weapons systems.

"Captain, we're receiving an incoming message from that ship," said the warrior at the communications station.

"Push it onto the speakers," Berven ordered.

"Unknown warship, this is the Confederate Navy heavy cruiser Cerberus. You are ordered to surrender, or be destroyed. You have 30 seconds to respond," said the disembodied voice over the speaker. The channel suddenly cut before Berven could reply.

"Talkative folks, aren't they? And who is the Confederate Navy?" Berven muttered. This mystery was going to have to wait.

Berven opened a shipwide channel. "All hands, this is the Captain. We've encountered a large, hostile warship of unknown origin. We're going to take it as a war prize. Continue to man your battle stations. We will be in combat shortly. Berven out."

Berven opened another channel, this time directly to Eric the Dour. "Eric, this is Berven. Il Mio Dieci will have to wait. I'm sending you the data on this new ship. We're about 20 minutes out. Launch your pods and board that ship. Warspite will try to keep them occupied while you're in transit."

Eric responded immediately. "Aye, Captain. Capturing a ship will be my pleasure. We'll launch immediately. Eric, out."

Within seconds, several dozen small pods began detaching from Warspite's hull and quickly moved away under their own power. Within two minutes they had all dispersed and vanished out of sight.

"Enemy ship is moving off, Captain. She's launching multiple ships," said the weapons station warrior.

"Fire first missile salvo and take evasive action. Let's keep them busy for a while with our faster speed and maneuvering," Berven ordered.

***

"They're launching pods from the ship's hull, Captain. Last count is at least 65," announced Delacroix. His eyes were glued to his screens, which showed a cloud of scan returns. "Tacnet is being updated with their plots, but they're so tiny we're losing contact with them right after they launch."

Without being prompted, Perez reminded everyone they were limited in mobility. "Captain, we've entered another uncharted debris field. There's too much interference to risk another FTL jump in here." No one was particularly surprised to hear there were uncharted debris fields that presented a navigational hazard. It happens fairly often, and they had jumped into an area where they knew debris was pretty likely.

Without glancing up from his screen to look at Delacroix or Perez, Ronin nodded slightly and ordered, "Launch Tomcats to hunt them down and destroy them. Link the point defense systems to the Tacnet plots and shoot them down if they get near."

Mueller looked at Perez at the ship's helm. "Lt. Perez, let's draw them away from the mining installation. Take evasive action as needed on your initiative."

Perez nodded. "Aye, Commander."

Ronin pulled up the Tacnet plot on his personal screen as Cerberus began to shudder slightly while the Tomcats stormed out of the ships launch tubes. The enemy ship, now designated Bandit 1 on Tacnet, suddenly changed course and speed, while launching a salvo of missiles.

"Aspect change. Bandit 1's revised attack profile now suggests they are trying to standoff and draw our attention," LeCroy announced from the tactical station.

Despite their impressive missile acceleration, Cerberus had several minutes until the missiles would arrive, so Ronin studied the Tacnet plot for a few more moments. The enemy ship was pretty distant and it was clearly capable of rapid fire and maneuver. It certainly did not appear to outgun Cerberus, but it was smaller and faster. At this distance, the nimble vessel would have little difficulty dodging railgun ordnance and most missiles.

"Captain, the pods have reappeared on our scopes! They're closing in on Cerberus," Delacroix said, interrupting Ronin's thoughts.

***

"This is Archangel, let's break 'em up," Sunderland ordered over the squadron commlink from the cockpit of his Tomcat. As he usually did on a combat mission, Sunderland had taped pictures of his wife, Amie, and their two young sons, Michel and Tomiah, to a part of his dash. Sunderland's eyes glanced at them and the images lingered in his thoughts for a moment while his Tomcat completed its hard turn towards the incoming pods. There were dozens and dozens of them, jinking wildly and moving incredibly fast.

Sunderland looked out the cockpit window to his right, where he could see his wingman. Bouncer was holding his usual position a mile off his right wing, flying slightly above and behind. At this distance, Bouncer's Tomcat looked tiny.

Suddenly, an alarm sounded and his attention riveted on his Heads Up Display as the first of the pods came within missile range. He acquired target lock and sent the missile on its way.

"Fox three!" Sunderland called out on the squadron commlink to let them know he was launching. Soon after, other calls echoed him. Pods began disappearing from the updated Tacnet plots as the missiles found their targets. There was an immediately apparent problem though. The pods were rapidly converging on Cerberus instead of the mining installation.

"Cerberus, we won't be able to stop all the pods before they intercept you." Sunderland called over a command commlink to the ship.

***

"Captain, the incoming pods are approaching from all points of the compass and Archangel reports they won't be able to stop them all before they arrive at our location," reported LeCroy from the tactical station. Tacnet had already made it abundantly clear where the widely disbursed pods were heading.

Before Ronin had a chance to respond, the ship began vibrating slightly as its point defense systems opened fire. "Lieutenant LeCroy, launch a salvo of jump bombs at Bandit 1."

LeCroy nodded. "Aye sir, launching jump bombs." He fired the weapons as he said so.

Tacnet showed the number of pods dropping rapidly as they were picked off from the Tomcats and the point defenses of Cerberus. While Ronin was looking at the screen plot of the battle, there was a sudden jolt.

"Pod impact on the ship's hull," Delacroix announced.

Mueller frowned. "Away the damage control party and have them report directly to me on what they find," she ordered.

Tacnet updated with new information just then. "Impact! Bandit 1 took a direct hit from a jump bomb that got through the debris field. No report on damage yet. Remaining jump bombs were destroyed in transit to the target from the navigational hazards," LeCroy announced. Bandit 1 was too far away to know how badly it might be damaged, if at all.

Ronin needed to know more. "Focus long-range optics on it and try to get a preliminary damage estimate until we have a chance to take a closer look when this is all over," he ordered.

***

Eric the Dour had little trouble exiting his small attack pod and finding a way inside the enemy ship. His pod had come to a stop on top of an airlock, and he used his Monosabre to cut through the lock. While the hull metal of the ship was too tough for a Monosabre to cut, the locking mechanism on the airlock was softer and more susceptible to the blade. His battleaxe was poorly suited for this assault.

Once inside, he waited for the airlock to cycle and then stepped into the interior of the strange ship. It was somewhat brightly lit, with light-colored walls and surfaces. He shed his air suit and tossed it disdainfully behind him. When he suddenly heard the sound of running footsteps outside the airlock room, he attached his Monoshield to his left arm.

Eric stepped into the corridor adjacent to the airlock, surprising over a dozen members of a damage control team that had skidded to a stop mere feet away from the frightening sight of a huge, bearded man with dirty blonde hair holding a shield.

Eric raised his Monosabre and roared, "For Ullr!" and slashed through the torso of the person nearest him. The preternaturally sharp monofilament blade cut through the tall, dark skinned female engineer so quickly and smoothly it was as though her body wasn't even there. She died instantly and her body parts fell to the floor, while Eric was already destroying his next victim.

The person in the back had just enough time to open the commlink node at their neck to say "This is the damage control party. There's enemy forces onboard!" before he, too, died a violent death.

***

The report over the speakers on the Bridge silenced everyone. "This is the damage control party. There's enemy forces on board!"

Ronin reacted instantly and opened a commlink. "Lieutenant Gustav, this is the Captain. Repel boarders at the locations indicated on Tacnet. Unknown numbers and armaments at this time."

Almost simultaneously, the repel boarders alarm klaxon began blaring, and the ship shuddered with additional impacts.

Gustav replied breathlessly, "Good copy. Repel boarders. Aye, Captain. Gustav out." Gustav had swiftly run towards the Echo team ready room as soon as heard the damage control party's message over the command commlink. After replying to Ronin, he closed the commlink and within seconds arrived at the ready room.

Echo team was already assembled and kitted out for combat because of the ship's alert status, and their facial expressions were hidden inside their exosuits. Nonetheless, the body language of several of them reflected surprise at Gustav's sudden appearance in their ready room. None of them had been connected to the command commlink, so all they had heard was the repel boarders klaxon piped over their exosuit's audio inputs.

"Echo team, repel boarders amidships. The data is uploading to Tacnet now. Move out and attack the targets I've designated for you!" Gustav shouted while he completed buttoning up his own exosuit. As was customary, Gustav hadn't fully sealed it so he could stay on the ship's air while he monitored his teams and the ship's sensors to stay abreast of the tactical situation.

Echo team had been seated in the center benches, which were positioned in rows forming a large square, in their spacious ready room down in Marine country. Individual cages containing each team member's gear and exosuit lined the outer walls. The room was filled with racks and gear, including many of their handheld weapons, while their bigger toys resided in the armory next door. An armory was directly connected to each of the team's ready rooms.

Amid shouts of "Aye, aye!" Echo team stood to and rapidly moved towards the unusually large hatch leading to the rest of the ship. The hatches leading to the ready rooms were triple wide to facilitate rapid deployment of the Marines in case of an emergency. One like repelling boarders.

Gustav briefly fell in with Echo team as they poured into the rest of the ship, and opened an all-team commlink. "This is Lieutenant Gustav. Echo is deploying to repel boarders amidships. Bravo team, deploy to the fore section of the ship and repel boarders as designated on Tacnet. Gamma 6 and 7, deploy directly to the Bridge itself. The rest of Gamma team is in reserve and will act as our QRF unless they are deployed aft if we receive any boarders there. Standby for further orders."

The Bravo and Gamma team gunnery sergeants immediately acknowledged the communication.

Using the power assist from their exosuits, Echo team rushed towards the outer amidships of Cerberus while Bravo rapidly moved forward in the ship. Echo wasn't far from the landing bays now. Each time Echo reached an intersection in the passageways that lead in the direction of the boarding, Gunnery Sergeant Kanagawa issued rapid-fire deployment orders. "We can't get a solid fix on the boarders using internal sensors, so we do this the old school way and scout. Each scout stay in contact and do not engage if possible. Use your discretion, but try to wait for backup first if you have the option. Help will be close by."

When they reached the first of three passageway intersections leading to where the first pod impacted, Kanagawa deployed a scout. Kanagawa checked Tacnet again and reconfirmed there was just the one recorded pod in their zone. They passed three small arms lockers where groups of crewmen had assembled.

Within minutes of the repel boarders klaxon, the entire crew of Cerberus had outfitted themselves with weapons. The inside of the ship had quickly become an armed camp, while the civilians had already locked down inside their designated compartments prior to the engagement and were out of sight.

***

Gunnery Sgt. Brett Mackey was running as fast as he could. "Gangway!" he roared as he approached the crew clustered around an arms locker. His external exosuit speakers were dialed way up, so he could be clearly heard above the commotion in the brightly lit passageway. For some reason, his senses seemed excessively attuned to the flashing red warning lights along the passageway, and the now somewhat muted sound of the repel boarders klaxon.

Behind Mackey came the rest of Bravo team. The team commlink was quiet, as they were in All Business Mode. Nobody boards Cerberus on their watch and lives to tell about it.

The team ran on, approaching the three likeliest locations indicated on Tacnet. At a large intersection, Mackey skidded to a halt before turning to face his Marines. "We're splitting up into elements from here.

Element 1, take probable target 1 on Tacnet. Element 2, take target 2. Element 3, on me and we'll hit target 3. Disburse!"

Since Mackey previously designated who was in each element while they ran, Bravo team seamlessly split into their assignments without further instructions. With cold, angry expressions hidden by their exosuits, Bravo team flowed down each passageway towards their targets that had infiltrated the fore section of the ship.

CHAPTER 24

SLAUGHTERHOUSE

Eric the Dour stalked along a well-lit passageway, his mood growing fouler by the minute. Warspite had been hit, badly, and he didn't know whether he would ever get off this strange ship he was now in. Further souring his mood, after the joy of the initial slaughter of the crew he had encountered, people had become scarce.

Eric paused near a sign and looked at it. *Auxiliary Damage Control,* he read to himself. Although he could read the writing on the sign, it was in a font that he'd never seen before. "None of the Factions use this printing style. Who are these people?" Eric muttered aloud. This ship was all sorts of strange and unfamiliar to him.

At the sudden sound of a weapon discharge down the passageway ahead of him, Eric ducked behind the transparent Monoshield he was carrying. A marvel of Solaran technology, the shield was made from monofilament forged by a superheated fusion reaction. It was lightweight and strong enough to be impenetrable by all known hand-held projectile weapons. That made it the perfect tool in personal combat and hostile boarding actions.

Bullets caromed off the Monoshield while Eric eyed the shooters through the transparent shield. A motley collection of crew members had quietly tracked him here and opened fire while he was distracted.

Eric smiled evilly and brandished his Monosabre with a predatory growl. Essentially forged the same way as a Monoshield, its preternaturally sharp edge enabled a man to cut through most anything not made of hull metal or forged monofilament. Bullets continued to ricochet off his shield as he began to walk towards the shooters.

To their credit, the crew who were shooting at him continued to pour on the firepower even though it was obviously ineffective. Eric laughed aloud as he approached within 20 yards, causing the shooters to pause and exchange uncertain glances. "Now you will die!" he roared as he suddenly charged. In the light gravity of this ship, Eric seemingly possessed superhuman speed and strength.

***

Ivar Haraldson cut his way through the closed passageway hatch, frustration evident on his scraggly face. In his mid 20s, Haraldson had been raiding for about a decade and the scars on his face and torso reflected a brutal life of violence.

He could hear the sounds of combat echoing throughout the passages. Shooting, cursing, unintelligible yelling and screaming all provided the terrifying audio soundtrack as he boarded this strange ship, but all the locked hatches were seriously slowing him down. Haraldson didn't know the ship's hatches were automatically locked down due to repelling boarder's protocols of Cerberus.

Pulling hard, Haraldson finally forced open the hatch and he stepped through with his Monoshield held in front of him to guard against the bullets the crew he encountered always seemed to be firing at him. Squinting down the passageway, Haraldson again spotted more of the ship's crew taking up firing positions in every adjoining hatchway, or nook and cranny. But they weren't dressed in the gray uniforms he had encountered so far. These crew members were buttoned up in some sort of odd looking midnight-colored suit with a skin resembling black water that weirdly didn't reflect much light.

This is different, Haraldson thought, grinning wildly at the new challenge. He raised his Monosabre and roared his favorite battle cry before charging at them. "Ullr!"

***

Gunnery Sergeant Mackey and Element 3 raced down the passageway to the hatch that Tacnet indicated the boarders were attempting to breach. As he raced around a corner and through a hatch that his suit AI opened just prior to his arrival, Mackey and Element 3 skidded to a stop at the sight of some sort of blade penetrating the next hatch. Pvt. Terry Allison (Bravo 5) had taken up a kneeling firing position next to him, with his mag-rail rifle carbine pointed down the passageway towards the next hatch.

Mackey and Allison traded glances before returning their gaze to the hatch. "Any of you guys ever see a knife that can cut through metal like that?" Mackey asked over the commlink for Element 3 as the rest of them positioned themselves near something to shoot around.

A chorus of "Negative," "Nuh uh," and "I got nothin', Bravo 1," replied to Mackey.

As they watched, the hatch soon was slowly pulled aside and a stout man with a scraggly face stepped through behind a transparent shield. He was wearing a crazy mix of primitive leathers with dark metal straps and studding. Stony muscles and veins bulged beneath heavily scarred skin.

"Uh, Gunny. This guy only brought a big knife to our gunfight," quipped Allison over the commlink, although he was too busy aiming his carbine at the intruder to look at Mackey while he said it. "Think we ought 'a tell him that?" he added.

Mackey snorted in response. "He'll figure it out soon enough."

Protected behind his shield, the intruder suddenly raised his weapon and roared "Ullr!" before charging Element 3. He was at least 30 yards down the passageway from them.

"Fire!" Mackey ordered, and the Marines unleashed a wave of bullets that merely ricocheted off the shield into the passageway. Mackey couldn't believe his eyes as the intruder moved with twice the speed and agility of a normal man.

The intruder nimbly bobbed and weaved with amazing swiftness to reduce his exposure to the bullets, but the intense fusillade from the Marine carbines finally stopped his progress and drove him back. "Bravo 5, switch to your Buzzsaw!" Mackey ordered.

In his team role as Bravo 5, Allison was the heavy weapons specialist. Shocked at what he had just witnessed, Allison quickly swapped the carbine he was also carrying with his Buzzsaw rifle that was magnetically locked onto his backside. The Buzzsaw was the heavy Marine infantry assault rifle, and fired far heavier caliber rounds. Unlike the mag-rail carbines, the Buzzsaw used liquid propellant for a far higher rate of fire, and was nicknamed for the buzzsaw like sound it made when throwing a wall of lead downrange.

The madman down the passageway charged again just as Allison completed the exchange. Allison opened up on the intruder before he took more than a few steps, and stitched a line of bullets across the shield. The impact of the powerful rounds caused the man to stumble and lose both momentum and his balance. He turned slightly in a desperate attempt to keep the shield between the Marines and himself.

It wasn't enough and the intruder was struck through the opening by a half dozen mag-rail rounds fired by the other Marines before he was able to swing the shield back into position. Allison swept the Buzzsaw back to his target and the heavy bullets again knocked the shield away before punching into the man and ending him in a gory display of firepower.

"Cease fire!" Mackey ordered. A sudden quiet filled the passageway while the disciplined Marine Element continued to search for targets. The ship's internal sensors updated Tacnet to show there were no additional targets in this direction.

Mackey spoke on the all team commlink. "LT, Bravo 1. I have an all-team sitrep."

Gustav responded immediately. "Send it, Bravo 1."

Mackey didn't hesitate and his voice carried into the helmet of each Marine. "Bravo team Element 3 took down an intruder that had some sort of transparent, bulletproof shield. If you encounter something like that, use a Buzzsaw or a grenade or something that can knock the shield aside for the rest of the fire team. Intruders seem possessed of unusually fast speed and mobility as well."

Gustav's eyebrows shot up inside his exosuit as he checked Tacnet to confirm that both Echo team, and Bravo team Elements 1 and 2 were all about to make contact at the same time. "Good copy, Bravo 1. All Marines, this is LT. Be advised by Bravo 1's report. Stay light on your feet, use heavier weapons. Make it happen."

Clicks over the commlink acknowledged the order. Gustav again tracked the progress of his men on Tacnet and the position of the hostiles when he entered another compartment and could suddenly hear the sounds of shooting.

Gunnery Sergeant Kanagawa was likewise studying the Tacnet display on the inside of his visor as he opened a private command commlink to Gustav even though they had entered the compartment together. "LT, Echo 1. Hammer and anvil or fox and hounds?"

Inside his exosuit, Gustav smiled at Kanagawa's tactical references. In Marine parlance, and hammer and anvil generally meant to trap an enemy against an immovable obstruction while the Marines served as the hammer. Fox and hounds simply meant to run down a mobile enemy.

Before Gustav could respond, the yelling and gunfire suddenly ceased and the Tacnet icon representing the hostile vanished.

By way of reply to Kanagawa, Gustav said over the team commlink, "Argh! Echo team, fox and hound. Move out!" The team surged ahead towards the last known position of the hostile.

Thirty seconds later, Echo team arrived to discover a gruesome scene in another compartment. Six crew members had been sliced apart, with a rapidly fading trail of bloody footprints leading from their remains to a ragged hole in the compartment wall that lead to a passageway beyond. The dead crew had been four women and two men. The new passageway the hostile had broken into ran the length of the ship.

After checking for an ambush, Echo team and Gustav entered the passageway. The faint trail of bloody footprints led in the direction of the Bridge. Gustav opened the all team commlink and tied in the crew on the Bridge. "Bridge, this is LT."

"LT, Bridge. Send it," came Delgado's crisp reply from the Bridge communications station.

Gustav wasted no time. "Bridge, the hostile has moved into the ship's primary passageway. Echo team is in pursuit. Direction of travel is forward, towards the Bridge."

***

On the Bridge, Marine privates Aldo Pena and Juan Diaz traded concerned looks. Even though they were in their exosuits, their body language said all that needed to be said when they heard Gustav's communication about the hostile coming this way.

Ronin thumbed his commlink button to respond directly to Gustav. "Good copy, LT. Hostiles inbound. Ronin out." He looked around at his Bridge crew, confirming that they were all now armed.

Seconds of silence ticked by as the crew concentrated on their tasks. The quiet was finally broken by Delgado. "Captain! Bravo element 2 reports hostile down and they've captured one of the pods."

"Threat assessment?" Ronin asked.

Delgado was listening intently to her earphone commlink as Ronin asked. She looked over at Ronin. "Element 2 reports negative, Captain. It's not armed."

"Acknowledged," Ronin nodded. Suddenly there was a burst of sparks from the ceiling as a heavyset figure dropped down to the deck next to Ronin's command chair. The hostile intruder immediately crouched, lifted a transparent shield and wielded some sort of sword as Gamma 6 and 7 opened fire with their mag-rail rifles. This all happened in mere seconds.

Bullets ricocheted off the shield as Ronin dived and rolled away from a slash delivered by the powerful hostile. Both Gamma 6 and 7 ceased fire and sprang forward as one from the hatchway towards the intruder who was clearly targeting the Captain.

Ronin regained his feet and immediately began circling their unwelcome visitor. His intent was to twofold: to make himself a more elusive target to focus on while also forcing his opponent to turn and face either Ronin or the Marines. This intruder chose poorly and swung his blade at Ronin, who bobbed and weaved just enough for the blade to miss and cause the attacker to lose his balance slightly.

Just as the Marines arrived, Ronin continued his motion into a spin where he launched a wheel kick that whipped over the man's blade and shield. Ronin's back heel impacted on the side of the man's head with great force, stunning him.

Gamma 7 grabbed the man's shield arm, only to lose his grip as the intruder ripped it away from the Marine while Gamma 6 tried to get a hold of the sword arm. The rudely uncooperative intruder made a sudden move and his blade whipped up to neatly slice off Gamma 7's left arm, cutting through the tough exosuit armor as though it wasn't there.

From behind the intruder, a mag-rail rifle suddenly fired, causing the man's eyes to go wide as he tried to cut down Gamma 6, who was still trying to get a hold of him. The intruder slumped to the deck with a large, wet bloody spot rapidly expanding on both sides of his torso. With the threat averted, the Bridge crew burst into activity.

"This is Lieutenant Delgado. Medical team to the Bridge. Two casualties, both critical," Delgado announced over the commlink she opened to the Sickbay.

"Affirmative. Team is dispatching now. ETA one minute," responded the slightly accented voice of Nurse Chrizanne "Anne" Abara. The fact that Chief Medical Officer Hirohito Taketa wasn't the responder from Sickbay told Ronin he was already busy with incoming casualties.

While Delgado called Sickbay, Ronin and Mueller helped Gamma 7 down to the deck.

Gamma 6 was also busy. He had rolled the attacker onto his stomach to cuff him, then he began applying field expedient medical care in the expectation that a live prisoner might prove more useful than a dead one. "Gamma 6 to LT," he called on the Gamma team commlink to Gustav as he was trying to stop the intruder's bleeding.

"Send it," was Gustav's reply.

"Gamma 7 is WIA. One hostile is down on the Bridge. LT, there's more. His sword cut right through an exosuit," Gamma 6 reported.

"That's good copy, Gamma 6. Passing that along," Gustav confirmed.

Gustav opened the all team commlink. "All teams, this is LT. Be advised, the hostile's swords cut right through our exosuit armor. LT out."

While he was issuing this update, Gustav simultaneously checked on Gamma 7's medical status by eye clicking an icon on the inside of his exosuit visor. It reported that Gamma 7's medical condition had been stabilized by his exosuit, and that the medical team from Sickbay was now arriving.

With the medical team's arrival, Ronin got a good look at their attacker. He nodded towards Commander Mueller. "He's so young!" he exclaimed, drawing her attention.

Mueller stepped back to look. "He is!" she said in surprise when she got a good look at the powerfully built, blonde, blue-eyed youth.

Ronan's commlink chimed in then. He answered it while watching the medical team load up the casualties.

***

"The Pirate? Seriously? Oh, geez, that's a terrible nickname," commented Echo 8, Lance Cpl. Hiro Gozen, though he wasn't facing towards Echo 2, Lance Cpl. Adrian Longman. The two of them had been positioned to guard a key intersection in the passageways of Cerberus so they stood facing opposite directions. It was a three-dimensional crossing, though, with two horizontal passages on the same deck level bisected by a crawlway passage at a 90-degree angle.

Neither Gozen nor Longman wasted time looking at one another while they passed the time with a conversation on a separate commlink. Despite carrying on a conversation, they both also paid close attention to Tacnet and the other commlink traffic so they were situationally aware of what was going on.

"Hey, you know the drill as well as I do. Ain't nobody get to pick a cool nickname out for themselves in the Corps. You just get tagged with one, and it's probably going to be one you don't like," Longman said in his down-under accent. Longman kept his head on a swivel, and was kitted up for all the close-quarters combat he could possibly want. His powerful Stinger rifle was attached to the back of his exosuit, while he held a mag-rail rifle in his hands. Several grenades were also attached to his exosuit.

Gozen hadn't kitted out quite the same as Longman. He held the standard mag-rail rifle in his hands, but for some reason Gozen had opted to attach a Firefly rifle to the back of his exosuit. Gozen still wasn't sure why he grabbed a Firefly instead of a rocket grenade. Probably because the thing looked pretty sinister.

"All I'm saying is The Pirate sounds like a bad nickname from a cheesy 'B' movie," Gozen snorted. He was definitely amusing himself by razzing Longman about the bad nickname.

"I'll take The Pirate over Gamma 5's nickname anytime. Has absolutely terrible taste in women. He only dates the kind of women who have more red flags than a convention of matadors," Longman grunted.

"Ha! I was wondering why everyone called him 'Olé,'" Gozen snorted.

"Yeah. Well-earned nickname, too, mate. Takes time for a new guy to the teams like you to learn the story behind everyone's nick ..." Longman was saying when he cut it short. A harsh noise down one of the passageways had drawn their attention to a locked hatchway about 40 yards down.

A shower of sparks suddenly exploded from the locking mechanism of the hatch. Their audio pickups on their exosuits transmitted a terrible, metallic screeching sound as they watched some sort of blade cutting through the metal hatch.

"Echo 1, Echo 8," Gozen said as he opened a direct commlink to Kanagawa.

"Echo 8, Echo 1. Send it," came Kanagawa's crisp response.

"Echo 1. Hostile located, this position. He's cutting through the hatch," Gozen reported over the Echo team commlink. While he reported the contact, their current location was already marked on Tacnet for the rest of the teams.

Nodding to himself, Kanagawa tersely responded, "Echo 8, Echo 1. That's good copy. Sending Echo Element 2 to your position now. ETA one minute."

As Kanagawa was saying this, the hatch burst open and a hard-looking man in dark leathers quickly stepped through behind the cover of his shield. He charged with a power and speed that absolutely shocked Gozen and Longman.

Both Marines opened fire with their mag-rail rifles, but the rounds merely bounced off the shield and merely slowed the intruder due to the hail of bullets. "Echo 1, Echo 8. We're fully engaged!" yelled Gozen as he leapt out of the way of the boarder's Monosabre, which left a deep gouge in the passageway bulkhead as it missed Gozen.

The melee that took place over the next minute was hard to follow. The attacker seemed to possess superhuman speed and reflexes, though the Marines in their exosuits did, too. Sounds of exertion mixed in with the deadly sounds of the Monosabre's passage, and the staccato firing of the mag-rail rifles when one of them managed to gain a bit of separation from the boarder. Soon the sounds of additional Marine boots soon joined the symphony of close-quarters battle.

Finally, the parties separated as if pausing to gather their breath, before the intruder sprang forward again with his shield raised in front for protection from the Marines' rifles. Gozen found himself on the backside of four Marines who themselves were positioned between Gozen and the attacker, with a narrow gap that he could see through.

Before the attacker advanced 5 feet, a brilliant blue streak of propellant exhaust appeared, traveling faster than eyes could follow. It originated from behind the four Marines standing in front of Gozen and now occupied the narrow gap between them. No one was quite sure where it terminated, because it blew through the attacker's shield and continued on to the attacker himself and the bulkhead behind him. The projectile penetrated several more bulkheads before becoming invisible due to the diffusion of its propellant contrail. The only remaining part of the intruder was his booted feet and his legs, which ended between the ankles and the knees. A reddish mist hung over the area where he had stood, and his Monoshield had a hole punched right through it.

As the Marines gaped in shock at the ghastly sight, Kanagawa and another small element of Marines came running up the corridor from behind their position. "Check on Echo 8," he ordered the Marine next to him as they passed by Gozen's limp body. Gozen had been slammed into the opposite bulkhead from the Firefly's recoil.

"What ... where? What happened here?" Kanagawa sputtered as he tried to make sense of the situation he was seeing.

By way of reply, Longman was already calling for repair crews, so he hooked Kanagawa into the commlink. "Damage control parties to my position. Multiple bulkhead breaches. Hostile is down."

Longman turned to look at Kanagawa for his report. "Echo 8 just mowed down this boarder with a Firefly."

Kanagawa just shook his head. "You gotta be freaking kidding me. Nobody in their right mind would uncork one of those INSIDE a ship!"

***

"Captain. This is Lieutenant Gustav. Remaining hostiles down."

"Acknowledged. Lieutenant, thank your teams for a job well done."

"Will do, Captain. My after action report will be on your screen in a few hours unless we encounter additional hostiles. Gustav out."

Ronin looked over at the tactical station. "Lieutenant LeCroy, status?"

"All pods destroyed. The damage control teams are removing the pods that attacked the ship right now, and other teams are working on repairing internal damage caused by intruders. Enemy ship appears to be adrift and is in an uncontrolled, counterclockwise spin along its axis. Arch Angel has deployed most of his squadron in a screen to cover our position. An element of Tomcats is approaching the enemy ship to make a battle damage assessment. ETA is ten minutes," LeCroy reported.

Delacroix interrupted when a muted but rapidly beeping electronic alarm caught his attention. "Contact! A ship squawking FFI recognition codes just jumped into the designated recovery zone. It's Bulldog 3."

"Captain, message from Bulldog 3. They have Dr. Wright aboard, and one KIA. One unaccounted for," Delgado said.

"Bring them into the landing bay. Let's get our people taken care of," Ronin ordered.

Ronin walked to the scanning station. "Lieutenant Delacroix, anything else on your scanners?"

Delacroix shook his head. "Negative. This field of debris is extensive and the data is being entered onto our navigational charts as it's discovered by the scans. Besides the enemy ship, the rocks and dust, and that mining colony, there isn't much else here."

***

Bervin wasn't sure when he lost consciousness, but he slowly became cognizant of regaining his awareness. The bridge compartment of Warspite was nearly dark, lit only by some of the red emergency lights. As Bervin slowly lifted his head, he noticed he was still strapped into his command seat and that was why he wasn't floating lifelessly like some of the others. The macabre, red-tinted sight of several broken but floating corpses were barely visible in the dim emergency lighting. Warspite's uncontrolled counterclockwise spin had generated sufficient centrifugal force to press the corpses alongside the outer wall of bridge about halfway between the deck and the overhead ceiling.

Bervin tried to call out for a damage report. All he could manage was a sickly croak followed by a sharply inhaled breath and some rasping hacking, which was caused by poisonous smoke and fumes in the thinning air. The daggers of pain in his ribs told the story that Bervin's ribs were shattered.

I won't have to endure this suffering for long. Death by combat is honorable, Bervin thought to himself.

CHAPTER 25

WEATHERED THE STORM

"**I**nitial pass on the BDA is coming in from the Tomcats. Sending to you now," LeCroy announced from the tactical station, using the common acronym for Battle Damage Assessment.

Both Ronin and Mueller pulled the BDA up on their screens at their seats and studied the images and reports.

Mueller tilted her head towards Ronin and murmured, "Looks like the jump bomb only had a partial impact on that ship." Her eyes never left her screen as she said it.

Ronin nodded softly. "Yeah. I'm not terribly surprised it wasn't a clean hit given these conditions. Large debris field, and a wildly maneuvering target moving at unheard of velocity. A measurable percentage of relativistic speeds even."

Now it was Mueller's turn to nod, although Ronin's comment about relativistic speeds caused her to briefly glance over at him with a cocked eyebrow. "If our scans were accurate, that ship was flying at about 7 percent of light speed. We've never encountered a large ship that fast before."

"Cerberus can fly faster on our sublight drives, but it takes a while to reach to those speeds. Out engine governors keep our acceleration to within the tolerances of our gravity compensators so we don't end up as bloody smears from the Gs," Ronin pointed out.

"Away mission to board our prize and take a look at their gravity compensator tech?" Mueller asked, a half-smile forming on her face.

"It's like you read my mind," Ronin remarked, slightly tilting his head towards Mueller as he did so.

"Captain, Bulldog 3 has arrived in the landing bay," Delgado reported, interrupting Ronin and Mueller's conversation.

"Acknowledged," Ronin replied.

"Are we in a hurry to capture the prize? I'm not getting the sense that we're going to rush right over there and look for survivors," Mueller asked, although her tone made it more of a statement than a question.

Ronin looked thoughtful. "We own the battlespace at the moment and now that our drone sensor screen is up, it'll give us plenty of warning if anyone wants to pay a visit to the enemy ship. Our BDA also shows that ship sustained critical damage and it's leaking atmosphere everywhere. What's left of her drives would have to be rebuilt from scratch in a fully equipped space dock facility, so they're not going anywhere. A few hours of time will eliminate most of any crew that might have survived the jump bomb, and our boarding party will capture the rest."

Prompted by an idea, Ronin thumbed open a commlink. "LT, this is the Captain."

"LT here, Captain. Send it."

"LT, prepare a detachment to board the enemy ship in a few hours. I want to let time work on our side to eliminate more hostiles before your arrival and make the boarding easier."

"Aye, Captain, we'll have a boarding plan worked up that'll include tactics to deal with those swords and shields we encountered," Gustav replied.

"LT, your men captured several of those swords and shields, correct?" Mueller interjected.

Gustav took the liberty of looping Alphonso into their commlink as he had already been speaking with him on another commlink. "Yes, Commander. I was already on another commlink with Lt. Alphonso now and am connecting him to this call. Lieutenant Alphonso?"

Alphonso didn't seem surprised to suddenly be commlinked into the call with the Marine Lieutenant, Captain and Commander. "Alphonso here. Is this about the toys Lieutenant Gustav is bringing to my Fabrication area?"

Gustav answered first. "That's affirmative. I'll be there in two minutes with a set for you to play with."

Mueller nodded approvingly. "Excellent. Try not to hurt yourselves with them. We are very interested in what they're made of and how they work."

"Yes, ma'am. So are we. I have a couple of mad scientists plus the ship's AI who are all kinds of eager to get their grubby paws on them," Alphonso noted.

Ronin had a little bit more he wanted to cover in this commlink. "Alphonso, I'm sending a boarding party to the enemy ship in a few hours after the situation has had time to simmer down. I'd like you to send a couple of your mad scientists along with some engineers from Lieutenant Lazarus' section for the purpose of looking at that ship's gravity compensators. Based on the sublight acceleration and maneuvering we observed, they may have a substantially superior system than we have aboard Cerberus."

Alphonso's voice did nothing to contain his excitement at the chance to get his hands on captured advanced tech. "Better compensators? Oh yes sir, with pleasure! I'll pass word along to Lieutenant Lazarus for him assign a few engineers to the boarding party."

"Outstanding, Lieutenant. Go capture us some advanced tech," Ronin replied.

CHAPTER 26

LESSONS LEARNED

A week later, most of the ship's senior officers met in Cerberus' main conference room to discuss their lessons learned from the encounter with the enemy ship they now knew as Warspite. Several of them looked fairly haggard from lack of sleep.

Ronin was all business. "Alright, everybody. Let's get to it. The unplanned First Contact with Warspite was rough. Most importantly, our AI solved Warspite's data encryption, so we have been combing through that ship's files.

"We know this ... Cerberus has found Solara, one of the fabled Lost Colonies. We know they're human and that after The Fall, Solara split into multiple Factions with rapidly shifting military alliances. The planetary regions controlled by each Faction correspond to one Faction for each of the seven continents surrounding a central jungle continent. We also know we had the misfortune to encounter the most warlike and violent of those Factions on the way to the mining facility. That Faction is called the Ullr, and they hail from a far northern continent of the same name. Notably, and we're guessing a bit on this, Ullr do not normally make outright allegiance with anybody, and they generally don't appear to like anybody. The competing Faction on the mining facility we are going to visit call themselves the Cosa Nostra, and they call their continent Italia."

Pausing for a moment to let his words sink in, Ronin looked around at the gathered crew, who were listening with intent expressions on their faces. They understood they were headed into a dangerous situation—a colony with a fractured society that had lacked a unified planetary government since The Fall.

Ronin continued. "Warspite's records are incomplete, but they speak of a time the Solarans refer to as the Dark Ages. This took place after the colony was attacked during the Fall and the jump gate was shut down to prevent more attacks coming from Earth. You're all cleared for top secret here, so I'll share this with you. We think we've already stumbled across the jump gate out beyond the edge of the Alioth system, but the Ullr records lacked information on where it might be found. Due to that ancient attack, the capital and largest cities of this colony were destroyed and the remains of Solaran society fractured into today's competing Factions."

Ronin turned towards the ship's Chief Medical Officer, Dr. Hirohito Taketa. "Dr. Taketa, I want to start with your report first so everyone has a chance to hear it direct from you." Ronin spoke as though he were giving both an order and an introduction.

Taketa cleared his throat and nodded in return. "I'll start with our casualty report. 31 dead on Cerberus, plus two from the crew of Bulldog 7, and 62 wounded. As you are all probably aware from the scuttlebutt about the boarder's unique weaponry, or having seen it in action firsthand, most of the wounded are missing limbs or suffered deep cuts, or both. The young intruder who was badly wounded and captured on the Bridge is recovering in sickbay, under restraint and heavy guard. My examinations of him and the other prisoners have yielded ... surprising information."

As he paused to take a breath, Taketa became aware of the drama he was unintentionally creating with his report. "Firstly, and my sense is this will be of great interest to Lt. Gustav's Marines, is that our genetic scanning suggests the Ullrians show significant levels of genetic manipulation as well as natural adaptations in their DNA. They are much stronger than the humans on Earth. Bone strength and density are much higher. Same for muscles. More efficient oxygen use. Stronger hearts to accommodate the stronger bodies. Faster and more efficient healing from injuries as well as a higher resistance to cancers and infections."

Gustav didn't want to wait to ask his question. "Doc. How much stronger are we talking? We definitely saw signs of great strength and speed during the boarding action."

Ronin added, "We saw it on the Bridge, too. I hit the intruder with a wheel kick to the head that would have easily shattered several inches of oak, but he was merely stunned for a few moments instead. A kick that hard would normally have dropped most humans like a hot rock."

Taketa nodded. "I heard about that, Captain." He then looked at Gustav. "Expect individual variances, of course, but on average they are at least half again as strong as Earth standard."

His utterance triggered multiple intakes of breath around the table. Cerberus was dealing with a race of super strong humans, and that could be quite dangerous.

Taketa continued. "We are patching up our wounded by either regrowing limbs, or fixing them up with mechanical prosthetics. The Ullrians also appear to enjoy regenerative healing powers about four times stronger than we have. Due to their strength and healing, we are keeping all of them heavily sedated while onboard. There's more. The same genetic scans have revealed they lack any immunity to the engineered virus that ravaged Earth in The Fall. It never made it here."

"Doc, will we infect this 'society,' for lack of a better word, if we come into contact with their peoples?" asked Commander Mueller. No one wanted to accidentally unleash a world-destroying plague, especially the same one that had already decimated one population long ago.

Shaking his head, Taketa said, "No, that plague burned itself out and disappeared centuries ago after everyone who lacked immunity to it died. The main strain of that rapidly mutating virus also mutated out of the ability to infect humanity. It's gone.

"Records aboard Warspite also noted there was a failed mass vaccination program on Earth in a last ditch attempt to stop the spread of the virus that actually did more harm than good. Since this vaccination information was solely gleaned from Warspite's records, obviously some flight traffic carrying that information made it through the jump gate for several years after The Fall had begun and before the gate was shut down.

"Apparently, the vaccine caused many more deaths a few years after being administered to the population. It had been rushed into production without adequate testing because of the scale of the emergency and the vaccine had long-term side effects.

"Those side effects that developed some years later were severe, including one side effect that left the population even more susceptible to a mutated strain of the virus along with other infections. Another side effect caused severe respiratory ailments, leading to early death.

"Ultimately, only the small percentage of humans who possessed a natural immunity survived, and they took up arms to protect themselves from the government's misguided attempt to vaccinate them during the chaos of a dying civilization. Eventually the entire vaccinated population died and with their demise, the conflict ended between the government and the unvaccinated survivalists. And we are probably all all descended from those unvaccinated survivalists."

As Taketa finished his report, he observed the intense interest in the faces of the other officers around the table. Since the Confederacy had no surviving records regarding the history of this incident, this was the first they heard about the ancient vaccination program that failed to stop The Fall from progressing back on Earth, or about the armed resistance their ancestral survivalists mounted to prevent compromising their natural immunity and to avoid falling victim to the injection's slow-acting but fatal side effects.

Ronin broke the spell that Taketa seemingly had cast over the assembled officers. "Lt. Alphonso, you have something interesting to report, too. Go ahead, please."

It wasn't often that the other officers encountered Alphonso, as he tended to spend most of his time with his staff of mad scientists down in Fabrication. While the department's name spoke to the ship's ability to make parts and components, the actual function of Fabrication went far beyond manufacturing—because the ability to make all that equipment required the ability to design it. A close-knit team of talented engineers, researchers, manufacturing crew and scientists who could print, weld, grow, forge, nail, hammer and glue whatever Cerberus needed populated Alphonso's Fabrication team.

Alphonso had also clearly been busy since the encounter with Warspite. Dark circles under his eyes spoke to long hours over the past week. Clearing his throat, he said, "Yessir. First item is Fabrication has been working with Damage Control to repair and replace the damage caused by the boarders. That was accomplished within hours of the attack.

"The difficult part as far as Fabrication goes is determining how they were able to cut through metal and exosuit armor using their swords and deflect projectile weapons with those shields. It turns out the answer is the same. Our AI tapped into Warspite's data and we learned what the material is that was used for those weapons, and that those weapons are called a Monosabre and a Monoshield. They were both made out of monofilament, but employed in different aspects.

"The Monosabre consists of a single strand of monofilament edge applied to a blade that also consists of millions of layers of monofilament stacked together to form the blade behind the edge. The result is an incredibly sharp, bladed weapon capable of slicing through most other materials at the subatomic level. The monofilament is so thin it actually cuts between the atoms to separate materials.

"The Monoshield is essentially the same as the blade, consisting of millions of layers of monofilament stacked on top of each other to create a super dense, yet incredibly light, shield capable of deflecting most projectiles as well as Monosabres. The technology used to create these weapons is simply brilliant. The blade is so sharp, that it takes a super dense material like hull metal to resist the cutting edge. We're working to devise methods and materials to deal with them."

Pausing for a moment, Alphonso couldn't help but see Gustav's intense interest in the monofilament weaponry. His Marines had already encountered them, and they needed to know more, fast.

Alphonso continued, "Secondly, we have analyzed Warspite's technical data on that ship's gravity compensators. Our preliminary determination is that system is roughly three times more effective than anything in the Confederate Navy, which allows those ships to utilize much more of their sublight drive power to achieve much greater maneuverability.

"Currently we do not yet know what it would take to upgrade Cerberus with it, but I suspect we would need to retrofit and overhaul major portions of the ship at the Argo Station Shipyards to do it. We'll get a better idea about that as we move forward and have time to fully analyze the situation. I also have an idea that I'd like to test regarding rigging up a Firefly with a small gravity compensator to reduce the recoil."

Lieutenant Gustav's eyebrows shot up at hearing there might be a solution for the Firefly's awesome recoil. Alphonso saw his reaction and looked at Gustav. "There will be NO tactical acquisition of the next prototype by your Marines this time, Lieutenant."

Guffaws broke out around the table. Everyone knew Gustav's Marines would find a way into the inner sanctum of Fabrication to steal the next prototype, or they would die trying. Gustav would never let Alphonso's direct challenge go unanswered.

"Message received, Lieutenant," Gustav said, although his tone clearly conveyed he was already contemplating sending an entire team of heavily armed, exosuited Marines to assault Alphonso's fortress within the hour.

Despite putting on their best poker faces, Ronin and Mueller couldn't stop half-smiles from spreading across their faces. Ronin looked at Gustav. "Lieutenant?" he asked, indicating it was Gustav's turn to give his report to everyone present.

"Yessir. You all heard the casualty report. Marine casualties in the boarding action were light. Gamma 7 lost his left arm in the defense of the Bridge. Doc Taketa is fitting him with a mechanical prosthetic so he can return to duty in a week or so. In light of the mechanical advantage that he will enjoy, my teams have already instituted a preemptive arm wrestling ban on Gamma 7.

"We are working up tactics and strategies to counter the unique weaponry employed by the boarders and we will be practicing them soon. Echo 8 is recovering from his injuries and is able to return to light duty while he heals up. All boarders were either killed or captured.

"Our own boarding action on Warspite went as flawlessly as any I've ever experienced before. Most of Warspite's crew were killed trying to reach Cerberus. Our jump bomb strike killed the majority of their crewmembers who remained aboard their ship died in or as a result of that strike. We captured a dozen of Warspite's crew, but they were nearly dead when we arrived and weren't able to put up any resistance. The Ullrians we killed seem to also have interesting names, like Eric the Dour and Ivar Haraldson."

Gustav's report was typical for him. Short and succinct.

Ronin pursed his lips slightly as he looked at Gustav. Raising his eyebrows, he pressed further. "And?"

"Captain?" Gustav suddenly looked as though he had something to hide.

"I understand a new nickname was bestowed ..." Ronin prompted. He wasn't going to let this go, and now everyone was looking at the two of them with more interest than usual.

Looking guilty, Gustav nodded. "Yessir. There was." Gustav paused, trying to figure out how to get out of this situation.

"You going to tell us, or is it some sort of secret?" Mueller asked.

Sighing slightly, Gustav surrendered. "Yes ma'am. Lance Corporal Gozen acquired a new nickname as a result of his actually uncorking a Firefly inside the ship. It's 'Gung Ho.'"

Laughter broke out around the table.

"Gung Ho Gozen?" Mueller snorted in disbelief. "Like in that TV show about the High Plains Drifters?"

Everyone knew the Drifters were a tribe of bandits who terrorized the northern plains of the Dakotas for a century after the apocalypse of The Fall. They famously had earned a reputation for unforgiving brutality and a lifestyle of high-speed raiding. The Drifters would attack without warning, roaring in on their ancient motorcycles and bastardized vehicles adorned with skulls and parts of their latest victims. Eventually the growing might of the surviving city-state of Sioux Falls ended the scourge of the Drifters as civilization slowly reestablished itself. The TV show Mueller referred to was a popular, long-running series that revived the history of the colorful bandits and made them famous across the planet.

"Oh geez. That's the cheesiest nickname I've ever heard!" Delacroix exclaimed.

Ronin winced slightly, but couldn't help grinning. In light of the term's history after the planetary apocalypse, Gung Ho really WAS a cheesy nickname. The High Plains Drifters themselves had actually used the moniker derisively to describe a person whose overenthusiastic and ill-conceived actions usually led to an untimely, and often spectacular, death or maiming. Firing a Firefly inside Cerberus to turn a hostile boarder into a gruesome mist certainly fit the meaning.

Ronin snorted softly before continuing. "Agreed. It's super cheesy, but I think Gozen might be the type of Marine who will take that nickname and make it his own. And frankly, the bestowing of nicknames is a sacred, and often creative, practice among the Corps. Marines are going to Marine. It's what they do."

Gustav nodded slightly, a half-smile forming at Ronin's articulation of Marines who Marine. It was the Navy's polite way of referring to the quirky and colorful personalities of the Corps who would chafe against the confinement of Navy rules and customs.

Ronin looked over at Dr. Wright, who was also present. "Dr. Wright, before we get to your report about the initiation of hostilities by Warspite and destruction of Bulldog 7, have you assigned a protocol officer to help build a relationship with the mining facility at Il Mio Dieci?"

Wright nodded. "Yes, Captain. Leroy Greene has already been involved in establishing radio commlinks with Il Mio Dieci. They are expecting our arrival soon after we finish with the remains of Warspite. They do not yet realize Cerberus is from Earth, but they're not stupid and know this ship is unlike any other in the system. They also know we are not approaching with hostile intent, and that we have the firepower to quickly eliminate threats like Warspite. My tentative assessment is they seem quite interested in building a relationship, although we might not yet be fully aware of all their motivations for doing so."

Ronin nodded. Wright's assessment was fair and considered, and Ronin welcomed Wright's still-incomplete transformation from the self-centered, clueless academic Wright had been when they first departed for the mission to Terra Station to a more tolerable member of the crew. At least the man was finally starting to grasp how a ship and crew functioned, though he still had a long ways to go.

Ronin wasn't thrilled with the assignment of the pampered, hopelessly entitled Leroy Greene to establish relations with Il Mio Dieci, but he recognized Wright had few options due to the small size of his department. Out in deep space, you dance with the partner who brought you to the party.

After Wright finished his report of the destruction of Bulldog 7, the meeting continued for a few more hours. They had a lot of planning to do to prepare for their arrival at Il Mio Dieci.

CHAPTER 27

SECOND CONTACT

At the same time Cerberus' senior officers were meeting aboard their ship, the small leadership team of the Miners Council on Il Mio Dieci were gathered around a table in their own conference room deep inside the asteroid. There were only 10 of them, and the current Council President, Franco Ricci, was speaking. Ricci was a serious man who closely watched out for his people's best interests. In his mid-30s, he was of average height with dark hair and dark eyes. He had the rough hands of a hardworking miner, which was exactly what he was.

"It's a ship called Cerberus. Our data on it is limited, to say the least. We've measured basic information like her dimensions and estimated tonnage. We've observed that Cerberus carries some sort of high-speed fighter squadrons. We have no data on propulsion and armaments other than to observe they clearly are highly advanced and very effective."

"What's the word from Don Morelino? Do the Families have any advice or help for us?" asked Luca Bianci, who managed the heavy equipment operators for the mine. Like Ricci, Bianci was a serious man and a hard worker who was focused on doing the job and taking care of his immediate family members.

Ricci shook his head. "The Administration ... The Families of Cosa Nostra were of little help. Raider 16 has been chasing after Ullrians and is just too far away from us to get here before Cerberus. There's not much Cosa Nostra can do for us much beyond offering what they imagine is helpful advice that would arrive too late anyway. The Families advised us to hope Cerberus isn't hostile, because that ship took down Warspite like it was an afterthought."

Bianci stared at Ricci for a few seconds before erupting in frustration. "That's it? Any idiot can figure that out." A wave of snorts and guffaws rippled around the table after Bianci's outburst.

Ricci held up his palms in a placating gesture that asked for some peace. "I know, I know. But we're out here on our own for now, and Cerberus did the universe a big favor by ridding us of Warspite. If Cerberus means to attack us, I doubt they would have bothered to establish communications with us or arrange a visit. If their Captain wanted to, Cerberus could easily blow us out of the skies. Thus far, their actions seem entirely consistent with a ship that means us no harm."

"Do we know which Faction that Cerberus ship belongs to?" Bianci asked. He had a lot of unanswered questions about their visitors.

Ricci shook his head. "No. And that's the thing. We can't tell who made it. None of the Family's spies have found anything related to Cerberus at all. The person onboard who spoke with our operator had a strange accent. The Family's spies also say each of the other Factions are also trying to find out which Faction could have built such a ship. There doesn't seem to be any records in any shipyard anywhere about a ship that even remotely resembles Cerberus. It's as though she suddenly appeared out of nowhere. "

The miners seated around the table traded concerned glances. "Nowhere? A warship that large? Impossible!" one of them exclaimed. Others nodded in agreement.

Bianci leaned back into his seat and clasped his large hands behind his head. "This reminds me of those old legends. Remember the prophesy about how Earth would reestablish contact with Solara someday? Something about an unknown ship that brings famine with it?"

Dead silence followed Bianci's comment. It was finally broken by one of the others at the table. "I think you're referring to the Bible's warning of the Four Horsemen of the Apocalypse. It's in the Book of Revelation. After the seals are opened to start the Cataclysm, the rider of the black horse brings famine."

Ricci interrupted. "Yes, but Bianci's not entirely wrong. There actually IS an old prophesy about a ship from Earth arriving after the jump gates are reopened and causing all sorts of changes on Solara. And this is a big, black ship that could be thought of as a dark horse of sorts."

Snorting, Bianci replied. "Yeah, but let's stay skeptical here. The old histories say Solara last heard from Earth when an ancient war broke out and our largest cities were destroyed before that mythical jump gate was closed. Since then, centuries of silence.

"Once we recovered and returned to space in this system, we've found no sign of anything that might appear to be a jump gate or anything else that would indicate Earth is real, with the obvious exception of the ruins of several large cities that are scattered around Solara. I think we should just prepare for the arrival of our guests in the normal manner that good hosts follow."

Ricci nodded. "Agreed. Let's break out the food and drinks and get to know our visitors over some meals. Find out who their Faction is, what their Faction wants and intends. Maybe we'll make some new friends?"

Heads nodded around the table. Faction politics were important among Solarans. All of them were intimately aware that forging an alliance with a powerful Faction could mean the difference between life and death itself. Ricci couldn't shake his strong feelings of unease over this mysterious and powerful ship that was coming their way. *Who are they, and why hadn't the Family's spies or satellites given them years of forewarning about Cerberus?* Ricci wondered to himself.

***

Ricci and Bianci stood together in the airlock's antechamber, their nervous energy making them unable to stand completely still. After trading glances, Bianci spoke first.

"Franco, I gotta admit, I got a bad feeling about this," Bianci said, using Ricci's first name since they were friends.

Ricci shook his head, tilting it towards Bianci. "Luca, none of us have a great feeling about this. But here we are. If Cerberus wanted us dead, we would already be dead. We saw what kind of firepower it has. If they wanted to take civilian slaves like the Ullrians do now and then, wouldn't Cerberus have sent over more ships than just this one?"

Bianci nodded now, too. Ricci's logic was clear. "Yeah, you're right. Cerberus wouldn't have had any trouble reducing us to dust if they were hostile. But that still doesn't make meeting them any more comfortable ..."

Bianci stopped when a bang sounded through the airlock hatch, followed by the sound of air filling the chamber and the spinning of the wheel in the center of the hatch. Seconds later, the hatch swung outwards and the two of them could see several faces through the opening.

"Permission to come aboard?" asked a strangely accented voice. It belonged to a tall, blonde, blue-eyed, human female who was the first person in the hatchway. She looked to be in her early 30s, was taller than most Solaran men, and was slimmer than the average Solaran female. She was also wearing a gray tunic and slacks that clearly appeared to be a military uniform.

Although he really lacked experience at this sort of thing, Ricci didn't hesitate. "Permission granted, and welcome to Il Mio Dieci!"

It never occurred to Ricci that shaking hands might not be a familiar custom to these strange new guests, so he extended his right hand towards the tall female. She didn't hesitate to shake his hand.

"My name is Franco Ricci. My friends call me Frankie. I'm the current President of the Leadership Council here on Il Mio Dieci. This is Luca Bianci and he manages the heavy equipment operators."

Smiling, the female nodded and responded, "I'm Commander Diane Mueller, First Officer of Cerberus."

Turning and motioning to those behind her, Mueller continued. "Allow me to introduce the party with me. This is our chief civilian protocol officer and diplomat, Dr. Winston Wright, and his subordinate, Leroy Greene. Behind them is Marine Gunnery Sergeant Toshi Kanagawa."

They exchanged a round of handshakes and quick introductions. Ricci and Bianci couldn't help but trade concerned glances.

"A Marine? Isn't that one of the types of military outfits on Earth we've learned about from the ancient legends? I haven't heard about any of the Factions resurrecting that old term from children's fairy tales," Bianci added quickly. He was hoping his remarks might prompt these visitors to drop some clues about their origin on Solara, but he certainly wasn't expecting the answer he received instead.

Mueller smiled softly. "Oh, we're not from around these parts. We're from Earth."

Ricci and Bianci stared at Mueller for a couple of seconds in the quiet that followed her statement, looks of sheer disbelief on their faces. Eyebrows raised high, they then looked at one another and burst out laughing.

Now it was Mueller's turn to look confused, along with Wright, Greene and Kanagawa.

"Um, what?" Ricci said after he regained control of himself. "I thought for a minute there you were trying to get us to believe in fairy tales about Earth."

Smiling patiently now, Mueller responded. "Cerberus is a heavy cruiser from Earth's Confederate Navy. I was born in Rothenburg, from an old country we believe was once called Germany." Nodding towards Kanagawa, she indicated he should speak next.

"I am from Kyoto, Japan."

Ricci and Bianci's smiles began drooping rapidly as Mueller nodded for Wright to proceed.

"I am from the Wilderness of what was once called Massachusetts, in the old United States," Wright said.

All eyes turned toward Greene, who quickly said "I am from Rothchild Heights, and am a summa cum laude graduate of the famous Diplomatic Institute in—"

"Thank you, Mr. Greene, that will be adequate," Mueller said, cutting off Greene. She couldn't help but roll her eyes slightly.

Ricci and Bianci looked confused. Mueller couldn't tell if it was from meeting strangers claiming to be from the Earth of childhood fairy tales, or from Greene's awkward egotism. It also had never dawned on Green that his credentials from some school somewhere weren't going to impress Ricci and Bianci in the slightest, regardless of whether they had ever heard of it, which was at best highly unlikely.

Ricci cleared his throat slightly, before motioning towards the exit with his hand by sweeping his arm that way. "If you'd be so kind as to follow us? We have so much to discuss. We stocked our main conference room with food and beverages, and it's equipped with all the data connections we have available on the mine."

Mueller nodded. "Perfect! Lead the way."

CHAPTER 28

SANCTUARY

"**S**anctuary is right where Ricci said we would find it," Mueller noted. She was standing at Delacroix's scanning station with Ronin as the three of them reviewed the data collected by the Bulldog scouts.

Ronin nodded absently, his eyes still riveted on the screen before replying. "Solara's version of Wayside Station, and more. A neutral ground space station in orbit around Solara and jointly operated by most of the planetary Factions. Absolutely stunning given what we learned about the open hostility between the Factions from the good folks at Il Mio Dieci."

Delacroix looked at them. "Space is so dangerous that even constantly warring Solaran Factions were able to agree to create a mutually acceptable refuge open to all. Even to Ullrians, so long as they behave themselves."

Ronin snorted. "Following rules isn't the Ullrian's strong suit."

Mueller cracked a slight smile at Ronin's understatement. "You think?" she jibed.

Now it was Ronin's turn to crack a small smile. "Sanctuary is obviously our next stop. It's the gateway to establishing contact with the Solaran Factions as well as literally being the largest gateway to the planet through a bottleneck in the system's asteroid fields."

Ronin looked at them directly now. "We'll approach using the standardized navigational data and communication protocols we received from Il Mio Dieci. Once Cerberus receives docking instructions, we'll dock at our berth. I want all weapons systems manned and ready, but our weapons posture will remain in their non-threatening positions. Questions?" he asked in a voice everyone could hear.

Heads turned his way around the Bridge, followed by a chorus of negative responses.

"OK. Let's make it happen, people," Ronin ordered.

***

"That's the ship that destroyed Warspite!" roared Anders Halfhand menacingly as he stared at the image on the forward view screen. Heads turned to look first at Halfhand, then to the view screen to see what he was talking about.

Surprised, the warrior manning the weapons station asked, "You sure about that?"

Slamming the remains of his partially sliced away left fist into the console in front of him, he nodded without looking away from the view screen. "Yes. It matches a auto-distress message that Warspite sent prior to her destruction. There was a optical picture of that ship in the message."

Halfhand's anger was plainly evident to anyone not already aware that his half-brother had been captain of Warspite. During his 10 years as captain of his own Ullrian longship Storm Bringer, Halfhand had acquired a reputation that was, even by Ullrian standards, wildly violent and rash with a long record of breaking sacred taboos. Now commanding a captured Zulu Faction patrol ship, Halfhand had decided to use it as a space-borne Trojan Horse to sneak into Sanctuary for a raid. The hacked apart bodies of the former Zulu crew had been jettisoned a few days earlier.

"We attack that thing in space controlled by Sanctuary, we can forget about raiding the space station," said the same warrior at the weapons station. He watched the two fingers of Halfhand's left hand tighten in barely controlled anger in reaction to his words.

Halfhand turned to glare at him before speaking in surprisingly level voice. "Destroying that ship is more important than finally raiding Sanctuary because that ship is strong enough to stop our raiders. Warspite tried to capture it, but she was too powerful and no one can approach without facing those weapons systems. Except right now, we're in close because of both ship's proximity to Sanctuary. We may never get this close again."

The warrior unknowingly pursed his lips as he nodded thoughtfully. Ullrians weren't afraid to attack a more powerful enemy, but being able to do it by sneak attack sure helped their odds for success and gaining honor for their boldness. He looked down at the weapons control screens of the station he was operating. "Range to target is about 60 seconds. They won't get much prior warning about incoming ordnance before impact. This captured tub doesn't have enough guns to win in a straight-up fight with that ship, so we have to target their engines. Take those out, and we may have a chance."

"How about their Bridge? Can we hit it from here?" Halfhand asked.

The warrior shook his head. "We don't know where that ship's bridge is, but I'm guessing it's in the center of the hull. Their enormous size obviously means it's a converted freighter with guns strapped on it, and the center of that huge hull is the most protected part of the vessel. This captured Zulu piece of crap we're driving doesn't have the punch to take out a Bridge that deep inside a ship that large."

Halfhand nodded. The warrior's statements merely confirmed what he had been thinking. He glanced at the plot of the two vessel's courses. "This is as close as we will get before our docking paths diverge. Sanctuary is parking us on opposite sides of the station. Target those engines and fire at will."

The warrior nodded. "On it. I have their engines locked. Firing now."

The captured ship began shuddering with weapons fire.

✳✳✳

"There sure are a lot of ships parked at Sanctuary, Captain," LeCroy noted without looking up from his Tacnet screens. LeCroy was keeping a close eye on Tacnet to spot the first sign of trouble. "There's a ship or three arriving and departing at least every day, too."

Ronin nodded slightly towards LeCroy. "You're going to be busy keeping track of all that while we're here. Keep your drones deployed," he said, acknowledging LeCroy's huge task.

Several minutes passed in silence while the crew monitored their instruments. Ronin had already brought the ship to Alert Two status, where the weapons were manned and ready, but with nothing out of the ordinary happening, he was starting to relax a bit. That ended abruptly when LeCroy suddenly barked, "Incoming weapons fire! Impact in 30 seconds."

Ronin looked down at his screen. The Tacnet displayed constantly updated information flowing in from their forward deployed drone sensor screen. There was just enough time to jump the ship before impact but the volume and caliber of fire were fairly light, so he made his decision instantly. "Sound Action Stations. Perez, roll the ship and get our engines out of the flight path of the ordnance. Lieutenant Anzio, return fire!"

Perez immediately punched in the commands to roll the ship and bring the primary railguns in line with the other vessel. Cerberus' drive engines went to full power and the ship began shaking with the power of max thrust. Cerberus suddenly shook with the impact of the enemy weapons ordnance.

"Captain, message from Sanctuary. They are advising a Zulu ship has fired upon us and are directing their patrol ships to intercept them," announced Delgado from her communications station.

"Acknowledged," Ronin said, not taking his eyes off the Tacnet readout.

"Captain, damage report. Minor impacts to the hull, and one of our railgun turrets took a direct hit. It's out of action. Three casualties, all wounded. Most of their ordnance missed due to our evasive action," LeCroy said.

Before Ronin could respond, Anzio said, "We have an updated firing solution. Returning fire now."

As she said this, the ship began shuddering slightly from the release of railgun ordnance.

***

"How did they react so quickly?" roared Halfhand as he watched the sensor readouts with dismay. Their attack on the huge vessel had been adroitly foiled when it turned out that ship was far nimbler and more heavily armored than they ever imagined.

"I dunno! The ship reacted so early, most of our shots missed, and then they just shrugged off the rest!" yelled the warrior at the weapons station. He hadn't detected the early warning drone screen that Cerberus had deployed.

They had barely managed to scratch the paint before the monster ship spat out a wall of angry hostility. It seemed to be coming from all over the giant ship's hull, and it was vastly more powerful than expected.

"Their return fire isn't like anything we've ever seen! Here comes the hammer!" the warrior yelled again. It had only taken a few moments of watching the sensors to realize that colossus of a ship packed far more fire-power than their captured Zulu ship. Or any other Solaran ship.

Seconds later, their ship was slammed from powerful railgun impacts. Halfhand had a momentary glimpse of bodies being thrown in all directions from the sheer power of Cerberus' ordnance before the lights and gravity went out. The bridge was cast into darkness, lit only by the occasional shower of sparks and a few panels of instrumentation.

Halfhand wasn't sure how much time passed before some of the emergency lighting snapped on. There were barely enough of those remaining to do more than illuminate a smoke-filled scene of horrors. Broken bodies from dead warriors who hadn't strapped themselves into a crash chair, and even from those who had. From his own crash chair, Halfhand could see several dismembered limbs slowly spinning and flowing with the rest of the untethered debris towards the exterior walls of the compartment. At first his stunned brain couldn't understand why everything was moving outwards, until he realized that effect was from the centrifugal force of his captured ship's uncontrolled spin.

Halfhand cleared the sudden congestion in his throat before he was finally able to croak, "Damage report!" There was no answer, so after a fit of coughing he said it again, clearer this time. It didn't matter; the still silence of the bridge compartment was the only answer he needed.

Using his uninjured arm, he untethered himself from his crash chair, and pushed off towards the navigational station. Catching hold of some now exposed wires, he pulled himself down and checked the pulse of the warrior who was still seated there. No pulse, and an obviously broken neck. Halfhand untethered the corpse and pushed it out of the way using his good arm so he could take its place. He wasn't quite successful and emitted a howl of agony as the corpse brushed against his broken arm and dislocated shoulder.

The station still had power, and was functional enough for Halfhand to quickly scan his ship's systems. There was an awful lot of red indicating each system's status. "What's still good on this ship?" he muttered, not that there was anyone left to hear it.

Halfhand's eyes grew wide as he took stock of his ship's condition. Weapons systems were down, not that they had been effective against the enemy ship anyway. Life support was not functioning in the slightest. Medical was offline. Engineering was likewise offline. Main engines weren't reading at all. In fact, the main engines had ceased to exist entirely. Air levels were dropping rapidly in the majority of the ship's compartments due to the extent of damage as the enemy projectiles had smashed their way through the ship and proceeded out the opposite side from where they had first entered the hull. Power reserves were dropping rapidly. Ship's thrusters were offline. The list went on and on.

Halfhand's blood ran cold as he concluded he couldn't even go out with a bang and make a suicide run at the enemy. One shockingly powerful salvo from Cerberus, and his ship was reduced to a ruined husk that wasn't going to threaten anyone. Halfhand belatedly realized that monstrous enemy ship was no freighter with a few weapons mounted on it, it was a purpose-built warship. He had attacked what he thought was a house cat with small fangs and claws, but instead they had provoked a Hellcat with anger management issues.

***

"Target neutralized, Captain," said LeCroy. He continued reading the scans sent in by the drones and never took his eyes off his screens while he continued. "Initial damage assessment ... heavy damage from our return salvo. Life support is down. Engine room took a direct hit and was destroyed. Primary engines are literally gone. They were smashed and torn right off the superstructure. Atmosphere leaks all over the hull, but they are rapidly diminishing as they run out of air. Ship is in an uncontrolled spin."

Before Ronin had a chance to acknowledge the report, Delgado spoke. "Captain, incoming messages from Sanctuary. They are apologizing profusely for any hostile actions in their airspace and are going to capture the remains of the ship and bring it in to Sanctuary ... they want to know what we would like to do with the enemy hull. Apparently their rules state an aggressor in their airspace forfeits property to the victim."

Ronin's eyebrows shot up as he traded surprised glances with Mueller for a moment.

Mueller spoke first. "Tell them we'll get back to them on that, Lieutenant."

Delgado nodded once and passed that along to Sanctuary, who seemed to anticipate that Cerberus would prefer to take some time to decide what to do with it.

"Threat assessment?" Ronin ordered.

"No threats detected. Sanctuary's patrol ships have assumed a defensive escort posture near Cerberus, Captain," reported LeCroy.

"Captain, if I may interrupt?" came the unexpected voice of the ship's AI.

"Please proceed, AI," responded Ronin.

"Captain, I have penetrated Sanctuary's communications grid and have been reading their message traffic. The rulers of Sanctuary are mortified and quite angry that Cerberus was attacked on their watch. They have warned the Zulu Faction they may impose a flight exclusion on their vessels as a sanction for failing to notify Sanctuary that a Zulu vessel had been captured and initiated hostile action in Sanctuary's airspace. The Zulu profess to be shocked, as they had believed the vessel to have been destroyed. Neither of those Factions know who was in command of the vessel at the time it attacked Cerberus," finished the AI.

"Thank you, AI. Please continue to monitor all communications and report any threats or developments," Ronin said.

The AI simply replied, "Affirmative."

Mueller tilted her head towards Ronin. "I hate to say it, but I don't think we'll get much more accomplished out here. Especially if we continue to block their flight paths like this."

Ronin nodded. "Agreed. Let's stand down to Alert Two and dock with Sanctuary."

CHAPTER 29

LAWYERS, GUNS AND MONEY

"Yessir, the survivors are getting lawyers appointed to represent them," stated Lt. Gustav. As was fairly common among the crew, Gustav had drawled together "yes" and "sir" into one word as he relayed the information that the handful of surviving attackers from the captured Zulu ship were entitled to legal counsel under Sanctuary law. "The good news is Sanctuary has permitted our Marines to guard the wing of Sanctuary where Cerberus is docked."

"Lawyers? Who bothers with lawyers in space?" Commander Mueller exclaimed in frustration. She couldn't believe what she was hearing.

"Commander, I for one wholeheartedly endorse the idea of legal representation for an accused regardless of where they may be located," admonished Dr. Wright from the other side of the conference room table. "It's the only civilized thing to do."

Ronin managed to keep his face impassive despite the overwhelming urge to roll his eyes. Of course, Wright would advocate a burdensome and inappropriate process over the swift imposition of justice out in space.

Ronin decided to move the meeting of section chiefs along and keep Wright busy for a while. "Doctor, do a search of the ship's personnel and identify crew members who might have the right sorts of experience to aid Sanctuary authorities in a prosecution." Then Ronin turned his eyes towards Lazarus. "Chief Lazarus, what's your timeline for finishing repairs on Cerberus?"

Lazarus traded glances with Alphonso before responding. "Captain, we can completely finish by tomorrow, except that Lieutenant Alphonso would like to take your temperature about an opportunity we currently have." He nodded towards Alphonso as he finished.

All eyes turned in surprise to look at Alphonso, who cleared his throat slightly before speaking.

"Captain, do you recall our conversation a while back about what it would take to install upgrades to Cerberus using technology we've tactically acquired?"

Ronin nodded, both as an acknowledgment and as an indication to proceed.

"Right then. Captain, we could utilize Sanctuary's offer of full use of their repair facilities to either repair the damaged mag-rail turret, or replace it with an improved, heavy version of Terra Station's x-ray weapon."

Ronin's eyebrows shot up and his head tilted slightly forward in surprise. "What kind of specs do you have for this change?" he asked.

Alphonso had anticipated the question. "The pulse cannon's weapon characteristics are quite different for obvious reasons. Due to our dark matter engines, we have far more power available than the folks back on Terra Station could have dreamed about, so our version can sustain repeated firing. This gives us greater range and allows us to cause more damage and to fire the weapon repeatedly. We can hit targets at twice the effective range of our mag-rail slugs because the beam hits the target so fast they can't evade it like they can with a slug. Rate of fire is four pulse beams per minute. The power in the beam is so high it will melt through 5 feet of hardened titanium armor with each pulse."

Mueller chanced a glance at Ronin's face when Alphonso finished. She could tell Ronin was sorely tempted with the possibility of adding an energy weapon to the ship, so she thought she'd advise him to be cautious. "Captain, we'd be reducing the mag-rail output by 10% in exchange for some experimental ray gun. Fleet Admiralty will have an absolute conniption if we do something like that."

If Mueller thought that was going to put the brakes on the experimental ray gun notion, she was quite mistaken. Ronin unexpectedly flashed an evil-looking half-grin instead.

"Oh, well, the Admiralty. Yes, we've never surprised the Admiralty before, have we?" Ronin quipped. His eyes focused directly on Alphonso. "Lieutenant, make it happen. I want that pulse cannon installed and operational. Draw on whatever resources you need to get it done."

Alphonso nodded. "Aye, Captain. On it."

"Captain, have you decided what to do with the remains of the Zulu ship that we hulled?" asked Dr. Wright, changing the topic.

Ronin nodded. It wasn't an inappropriate question, and he had been pondering what to do with it as well. "Yes. We give it to Sanctuary to do with as Sanctuary sees fit. It's valuable to Sanctuary, but is just a burden to us as we don't have a use for it."

Wright nodded. "Captain, may I inform Sanctuary about our gift then?"

"Yes, please do. Offer it to them instead of telling them we're giving it to them, just to be diplomatic. Maybe we'll make more friends here at Sanctuary." Ronin replied.

***

"Rumor is Lieutenant Alphonso's mad scientists are hard at work modifying the ship's weapons," said Lance Corporal Gozen. He and Pvt. Julio Gonzales had drawn Echo team's guard-duty shift inside the wing of Sanctuary that led to where Cerberus was docked.

"What, like a starship-sized Firefly or something?" Gonzales asked, his interest piqued slightly. Echo team had been patrolling and guarding this position for nearly a week, and the boredom was palpable even through their exosuits. "Imagine the recoil that would have!"

Both of them snickered slightly, until it was interrupted by a commlink from Lieutenant Gustav. "Echo 8, Echo 6. We've received a message from Sanctuary's operations center. They've requested assistance with a disturbance in another wing from a ship that just docked there. When your replacements arrive, you are to follow the routing information appearing on your Tacnet displays, observe and report. Further information follows as we receive it."

Gozen and Gonzales already could see the route to the other wing on Tacnet, as well as the constantly updated location of their incoming replacements. The replacements were moving fast and would arrive in about 30 seconds.

Gozen responded as the ranking Marine. "On it, LT. Replacements are almost here. We'll shove off as soon as they've arrived. Echo 8 out."

Gonzales and Gozen occupied the seconds before the replacements' arrival by re-checking some their weapons and equipment. "Everything checks out, Echo 6. Here they are, let's move," Gozen ordered.

Trading acknowledging waves with the replacements as they moved into position, Gozen and Gonzales quickly moved out. Their exosuits enabled them to resist the higher gravity and move with shocking speed.

Minutes passed as they traversed the wing of Sanctuary where Cerberus was docked. "Geez, it's easy to know how long this station's wings are, but it's another thing entirely to fully comprehend that each wing is well over a mile in length," Gonzales said to break the commlink silence between himself and Gozen.

"Kind of reminds me of their own version of an Argo Station Shipyard," Gozen replied, puffing with the effort of moving. The extra gravity was starting to wear them down despite the powered assistance of their exosuits.

As they approached the Sanctuary's center hub, where the wings jutted from like spokes, their external speakers conveyed the distant sounds of panic, weapons fire and screams. Then their commlink returned to life with the voice of Lieutenant Gustav.

"Echo 8, Echo 6. This is LT. Mission change. I was just advised our junior protocol officer, Leroy Greene, is trapped and needs rescue from a hostile boarding force. Go to his location and bring him back to Cerberus. LT out."

The route on their Tacnet displays changed slightly, which brought both Gozen and Gonzales to a temporary halt while they studied it for a few moments to locate Greene's beacon. Both couldn't help but note that the sounds of panicked civilians were rapidly growing louder.

"Echo 8, there's too much interference in here and those intermittent blips on Tacnet are making me unsettled. Suggest we launch a Butterfly drone to scout ahead while we travel," Gonzales said.

Gozen nodded. "Your comfort is the Marines top priority Echo 6. Let fly. We need a clear picture of what's heading our way."

Gozen obviously was already thinking the same thing as Gonzales. Apparently. so was Captain Ronin, because Tacnet suddenly indicated Cerberus' defensive status upgraded to Alert Two with the ship's action stations manned and weapons hot.

Gonzales launched the tiny drone and set it to scout ahead of them. The two of them moved more cautiously now, weapons in their hands. It wasn't long before the Butterfly transmitted a horrific scene of panicked civilians scrambling to stay ahead of an advancing front of shielded, Monosabre wielding savages. The attackers didn't seem overly picky regarding whether they killed or captured a civilian.

"Ullrians again!" Gozen muttered to himself. Just then, the commlink with Lt. Gustav made them jump inside their exosuits.

"Echo 8, LT. Confirm status, weapons hot?" Gustav said. He was also watching the video feed from the Butterfly drone and was double checking on his men.

"LT, Echo 8. Confirmed. We'll make enemy contact in a few minutes after that wave of oncoming civvies passes by," Gozen responded. He didn't sound highly optimistic, and Gustav noticed. Gonzales nodded in silent acknowledgment of Gozen's mood.

Gustav wasn't willing to give up the mission this early, but he also wasn't willing to spend his Marines lives in a stupid and futile endeavor, either. "Echo 8, Echo 6. Remember our Golden Rule ... 'Don't do nuttin' stupid.' If there's no opportunity to retrieve the package, break contact and get your butts back here. We'll leave a light on for you."

Leaving "a light on" was Gustav's way of saying the two of them would be headed back into a weapons hot zone where there was a decent chance someone could light them up with a rifle, or worse.

Gozen and Gonzales traded a look. "LT, Echo 8. Roger that." On a separate commlink he said for Gonzales' ears only, "Hopefully neither of us has stepped on anyone's toes lately."

Gonzales nodded. "No promises. The Good Lord says I'll be fine, but he's not too sure about your chances."

Gozen chuckled. "Put in a good word for me. See how it plays out." He looked around and abruptly changed the subject. "You know, there's too much light in here."

Gonzales stopped, and looked around in confusion. "Meaning?" he asked, drawing out the word. There were already civilians streaming past their current position now.

"We stop here, and place small charges around the lighting panels in this section. After the wave of civvies crests and the Ullrians arrive, we make this section go dark. Try to breach a gap in their line and sneak through."

"What, you brought some party favors along?" Gonzales asked, surprised at Gozen's armament choices for guard duty. His eyes quickly inventoried the extra kit on Gozen's suit, noting the tube attached to his back and extra pouches lining his utility belt. He had not really taken notice of them before.

"Never bring butter knives to a gunfight, Echo 6. Take these," Gozen said as he handed Gonzales several of those pouches.

Gonzales' broad smile couldn't be seen through his inky black suit's dark visor, but his body language spoke volumes. "Why Echo 8, that sounds positively underhanded and nearly dishonorable."

"You love it then?" Gozen quipped.

Gonzales did. "Like my own dear mother. I'll set boomsticks on that half, you take this half?"

Gozen nodded. "Let's make it happen. Tacnet says the crest will be in five minutes."

They worked quickly. Gozen's thoughts were nearly drowned out by the screaming of civilians and gunfire from the Sanctuary security forces as they were being pushed back towards their current position.

"Charges ready! Enemy contact forward!" yelled Gonzales over the commlink. He had climbed on top of a table and was already shooting his mag-rail rifle over the heads of the station security forces, who were rapidly falling to the advancing Ullrians' Monosabres. Blood was everywhere, and the wing was filling with light smoke from various weapons and small fires that were appearing due to the firefight.

"LT, Echo 8. There must be hundreds of them! Ullrian tangos have reached infestation status here!" yelled Gozen over the commlink. Even inside his exosuit, his voice was nearly drowned out by the thunderous *brrrrrrrt* sound of his buzzsaw rifle.

Both Gozen and Gonzales retreated slowly to lead the enemy to where they wanted them. Their accurate fire quickly cut down two dozen Ullrians. It was unclear whether it was the act of ending a batch of Ullrians, the firing of the mag-rail rifle, or the thunder of the buzzsaw, which also attracted dozens more towards their position.

"Echo 8, Anytime!" called Gonzales. He was getting very uncomfortable with the proximity of all these angry Ullrians and it was showing through the rising pitch of his voice.

Gozen didn't need additional encouragement, and he triggered the charges. Over a dozen charges ignited simultaneously, shattering the lighting panels and throwing this section of the wing into darkness. The sound of ear-splitting explosions rolled down the wing as thick smoke roiled from holes in the wall panels that Gozen had mined. Once their exosuit visors seamlessly transitioned to a combination of infrared and sensor vision, Gonzales could not help but notice the heavy damage from the more powerful detonations had occurred along Gozen's side of the wing. There were also dozens of shattered Ullrian corpses on the side of the wing that Gozen had mined with boomsticks.

In the dark, smoky and relative quiet that immediately followed the detonations, Gonzales commlinked Gozen. "Say, uh, Echo 8. Get a little frisky with that boomstick over there? Looks like you were trying to breach a hull or something."

Gozen snorted. "Just following the 'P for Plenty Formula.' Check it out. Tacnet re-plotting has updated with the Butterfly's new scans. The way is relatively clear on this route. Let's move out before they recover and plug the gap."

As they quickly advanced through the smoke-filled, darkened, temporary gap, Gonzales muttered to himself, "Our boy Gung Ho seems to thinks EVERY job is a man's job. He overkills everything."

Even though Tacnet showed the advancing front of Ullrians wasn't deep, they still encountered several savage warriors who were trying to recover their senses after the blasts. The smoke and lack of light made it difficult for them to do so.

Gozen soon realized there was a group of three Ullrians blocking their path through the dark zone, but it was by coincidence instead of by design. Without stopping to determine whether the three even knew what they were doing, Gozen took advantage of the situation because his visor's internal display clearly showed the three had lost their shields.

Gozen scythed them down with a fusillade from his buzzsaw. The high-velocity, large-caliber rounds from his heavy Marine infantry assault rifle and its high rate of fire left dozens of angrily punched holes through their corpses as they were flung back from the impacts. It was over so quickly Gozen had scarcely paused before continuing on.

Despite being blinded in the darkness and smoke, those Ullrians not too stunned and disoriented from the blasts began to hunt the sound of the buzzsaw. It didn't take a genius to figure out there was an infiltrator through the breach in their line. They began to call out to one another, using sound to coordinate themselves.

Gonzales was first to spot their next obstacle. He had passed Gozen while he was busy hosing down the unlucky trio. Gonzales paused, and then opened the commlink with Gozen.

"Echo 8, Echo 6. Contact front. Two dozen tangos. Distance about 40 yards. I can hear them coordinating by audio through my external speakers. How copy?"

"Echo 6, that's good copy. I see them now too. How are you fixed for grenades?" Gozen asked. He had linked back up with Gonzales by now and likewise stopped.

Gonzales was indeed packing multiple grenades. "Echo 8, I like where you're going with this. You want to sync some pineapples and leave them a parting gift?"

Gonzales had referred to the grenades using an ancient slang term, "pineapples." The word was in use during the 20th century, when some grenades had resembled the fruit. It had inexplicably managed to survive, though the term's origin had been long forgotten because of The Fall.

"Echo 6, that's affirmative. Grenades are synced. Prepare to throw on ... Three. Two. One. Throw!" Gozen ordered.

Using their exosuit power and guidance system to compensate for the extra Gs, they aimed their grenades to land exactly on the somewhat separated spots that Gozen had designated on Tacnet.

Gozen had set both grenades to detonate 3 feet above the deck for maximum impact. They exploded with catastrophic effect and shredded dozens of Ullrians. Their screams and moans filled the air, which only served to draw in dozens more of them.

Both Gozen and Gonzales opened fire with their rifles and Ullrians began to target the source of their gunfire. Gonzales immediately realized they weren't able to down enough of them as they advanced behind their shields in the dark.

"Echo 8, there's too many of them! I ..." Gonzales yelled into the commlink.

Gozen cut him off. "Less talking, more shooting!"

Gozen was desperately looking for a way out of this trap when he noticed a power coupling for recharging heavy freight machinery off to his right. His visor had highlighted it as one heat source among many in the station's wing so he was able to see it through the dark and heavy haze, but he hadn't focused on them until they had become desperate.

"Echo 6, get down!" Gozen shouted as he turned his buzzsaw in the direction of the coupling, which was at least 50 feet beyond where Gonzales was standing in between Gozen and the coupling.

Not understanding why Gozen commanded him to get down, Gonzales nonetheless recognized he had to act immediately because it was an order. Without hesitation he dropped like a stone to the deck. Angry sounding Buzzsaw bullets ripped the air over his head and thudded into the power coupling beyond.

Because of the darkness and skeins of smoke, Gozen hadn't seen that some of the freight was still in canisters on the hauler that had been recharging. His bullets also punched through the canisters, which left large holes in them. The gas that had been in those canisters escaped. It quickly formed a colorless cloud that dispersed away from the Marines and headed towards the approaching, menacing Ullrians.

Unaware of the gas discharge and too busy to worry about it even if he had known, Gozen fired a second burst as the coupling had survived the first bullets. This time his shots caused the coupling to emit a long, horizontal fountain of sparks and electricity that stretched all the way to the wall 50 yards away. It would stop any Ullrian pursuit that tried to pass through. It would also blind the Ullrians since their eyes had adjusted to the pitch black and they didn't have the advantage of self-adjusting exosuit visors to protect their eyes.

Knowing their exosuits would also protect them from the sparks and electricity, Gonzales began to stand up so they could sprint through into the unoccupied space beyond. "We're in business! Let's ..."

The colorless gas cloud intersected with the fountain of electricity and ignited a fuel-air bomb. The shock wave smashed down both Marines and it was followed by an absolutely scorching wave of heat and fire.

The resulting explosion rocked the entire wing. A firestorm spread in every direction down the station wing and burned up most of the air for a short distance. The deck undulation was so powerful that everyone was thrown down.

Several minutes later, Gozen regained consciousness. He checked his exosuits vitals. Internal temperature quickly dropping to normal, and the armor had deflected the worst of the shock wave. He had nearly been baked alive, except for the protection provided by the exosuit.

A hand entered Gozen's vision, reaching towards him in the universally recognized gesture that conveys an offer to help a person back to their feet. It was Gonzales.

"Echo 8 ... I'm telling the station owners to put the repair bill on your tab." Gonzales nearly grunted the quip as he was still trying to shake off the impact of the blast wave.

Gonzales surved the shocking aftereffects. The area where the Ullrians who had been swarming towards their position had been transformed into a charnel house of immolated meat corpses that were emitting smoke and burnt fluids. Beyond that was a gore-strewn field of shattered wreckage, jagged metal, and more corpses. Hundreds of Ullrians had died ghastly deaths, their shields offering little protection against the shock wave and firestorm. In this gruesome engagement, the Marine's exosuits had made the difference between life and death.

CHAPTER 30

CERBERUS

The entire ship juddered as if it had just been hit by incoming fire. Ronin immediately looked over to LeCroy at the tactical station for an explanation.

"Negative incoming fire, Captain. Tacnet indicates a massive detonation originating at the last known location of our rescue element that was sent after Greene. No incoming threats to Cerberus," LeCroy reported.

"Sound 'Action Stations,' LeCroy, let's upgrade our defensive posture." Ronin ordered. As he was speaking, the ship's alarm began its muted blaring on the Bridge, and calling the remaining crew to man their battle stations.

"Captain, ship's sensors are confirming a massive explosion inside our wing of Sanctuary station. There appears to be many casualties and a severe, but temporary, depletion of breathable air. Interior temperature of this wing jumped several hundred degrees, but it's dropping back now as the station's life support system is still online," Delacroix added.

Before Ronin could respond, his commlink node chimed with an incoming message from Lieutenant Gustav down in Marine country. Ronin tapped the commlink node and said, "Ronin here."

"Captain, this is Lieutenant Gustav. Our Echo team rescue element was engaged by enemy tangos as they tried to infiltrate behind their lines into their rear area. They report moving forward again now that the way has been cleared. They left behind hundreds of dead Ullrian warriors. I'm detailing Bravo team to round up any surviving Ullrians and secure this wing."

Commander Muller traded glances with Captain Ronin while they remained in their seats on the Bridge. Her eyebrows rose as she noted, "After a gigantic blast like that, Lance Corporal Gozen might have some competition for that "Gung Ho" nickname."

The commlink with Gustav was still open. He responded to Commander Mueller directly, thinking that her comment was directed to him. "Commander, that blast WAS caused by Gung Ho Gozen. He's leading the rescue element."

Guffaws and sounds of amazement erupted around the Bridge. Ronin raised his hands with the palms upraised and said, "Quiet down, people." Then Ronin replied to Gustav.

"Lieutenant, I'm going to reach out to the station operations center and ask if they need additional assistance beyond Bravo team securing this wing. In the meantime, keep Gamma in a QRF role until we hear otherwise."

"On it, Captain. Gustav out."

Ronin looked at Mueller. "Lance Corporal Gozen is certainly living up to his nickname. Once Gozen engages an enemy, he leaves behind a trail of devastation."

Mueller snickered.

Lieutenant Delgado interrupted. "Captain, I have Sanctuary operations on the commlink. They'd appreciate a word with you."

Trading glances, Ronin and Muller's eyebrows rose in a mirror image of one another. Ronin nodded toward Delgado. "Put them through, Lieutenant."

The audio/video commlink screen at Ronin's station displayed the image of a dark-haired man with dark skin and eyes and a stern-looking visage.

"Captain Ronin? This is the station duty officer. I understand you've offered additional assistance?"

"We have. What can we do for Sanctuary station?"

The officer on the screen nodded to someone off-screen, then a tactical map of Sanctuary replaced his face. His voice continued to narrate the video imagery. "Captain, the highlighted section of this map shows the current docking location of the ship where the Ullrians came from.

It seems that the previous attack you foiled on your way to the station wasn't the only attempt to use captured ships as a Trojan horse to sneak their warriors aboard.

"This is a new tactic by the Ullrians and we have started perfecting a responsive security protocol that should prevent this tactic in the future. Now that your wing has been substantially cleared of the Ullrians, our internal security forces have been able to rally and are engaged with them in other areas of Sanctuary. We will root them out, but would like your assistance to eliminate their ship to deprive them of the resource that it is. The ship has left docking and is maneuvering to dock at another wing to start the boarding action all over again."

Ronin looked over to LeCroy at the tactical station, an unspoken question in his eyes. LeCroy nodded back at Ronin, indicating that the ship was already plotted as a target on the ship's Tacnet. Ronin's eyes returned to the screen, which again displayed an image of the duty officer.

"It will be our pleasure," said Ronin. "Please advise your security forces that two of our Marines are traversing the interior of Sanctuary to rescue one of our crew who is trapped in the fighting. I'll have their locations sent to you."

The duty officer nodded. "Thank you, Captain. We will be extremely grateful, and I'll alert station security to their presence so we can avoid a friendly fire incident. Sanctuary out."

Ronin opened another commlink with Lieutenant Gustav, who answered immediately.

"Yes, Captain?"

"Lieutenant, Sanctuary station has asked for our assistance to stop the Ullrians from repositioning their ship and opening up another front to continue their boarding action. Is Bravo now in position to hold this wing while Cerberus engages the enemy ship?"

Gustav's eyes quickly scanned Tacnet on the inside of his exosuit visor before he responded. "Aye Captain, they're arriving now. I'll inform Gamma 1 that Gamma team's QRF role may also include a boarding action if need be. Be advised, I've shifted position and am on-site inside our docking wing of Sanctuary."

Ronin nodded, even though Gustav couldn't see it over the commlink. "Noted. Cerberus Actual, out."

"Enemy ship has indeed left the dock and is pulling away from the station, Captain," Delacroix reported.

Ronin issued rapid-fire orders. "Let's seal the hatches and sever the docking collars. Spin up the ships' drives." He turned to look at the helm station. "Lieutenant Perez, plot an intercept of the enemy ship and get the course laid in."

In less than two minutes, Cerberus quickly pulled away from Sanctuary.

"Captain, aspect change on the enemy ship. They've detected our departure and are running instead of moving to another section of Sanctuary!" Lt. Delacroix announced.

"Continue our interception," ordered Ronin in a flat voice.

"Aye, Captain. Changing course accordingly," responded Perez.

The roar of the massive engines of Cerberus could now be heard inside the ship as Perez brought them to full thrust. Everyone could feel the conflicting pull of the ship's internal gravity dampeners fighting to overcome full thrust of the sublight drives.

"We are slowly gaining on them, Captain. They'll be inside our maximum firing range in five minutes, but there will be plenty of time for them to evade our mag rail slugs at that distance. Jump bombs are advised," LeCroy reported.

Ronin was about to respond when the ship's AI interrupted. "Captain, there is another option. Lieutenant Alphonso has completed installation and testing of the pulse cannon. It's now online and has a targeting solution if you're interested in giving it a try."

THAT report surprised the entire Bridge crew. All eyes turned to look at Ronin.

"Are we sure it's safe to operate?" Ronin asked, his voice doing little to hide his interest.

Alphonso's voice surprised everyone, since he had just appeared on the Bridge and no one noticed due to all the commotion. "Yessir. It's already passed all our testing procedures. I was on my way to tell you when the current fracas started."

Mueller murmured, just loud enough for Ronin to hear, "Hopefully it doesn't have a recoil like a giant version of one of his original Fireflies."

Ronin glanced at Mueller, a half-smile quickly appearing. "Thank you Lieutenant Alphonso." His eyes flicked over to LeCroy at the tactical station. "Lieutenant LeCroy, do you have fire control over the pulse cannon?"

LeCroy nodded. "Affirmative, Captain. Lieutenant Alphonso just transferred control to my station."

"Then target the enemy ship's engines and fire two pulses of the pulse canon when we're in range," Ronin ordered.

"Affirmative. We're already in range. Firing now. First pulse is away." About fifteen seconds later, LeCroy announced the second shot. "Second pulse is away." Other than his announcement, there wasn't any sensation that Cerberus was firing on another vessel.

Delacroix was intently staring at his sensor displays. "Captain, acceleration of the enemy ship has stopped. Sensors are reporting possible fires or some other sort of massive heat surges inside the ship. I'm not sure what to make of these readings, but it's possible the entire ship lost power. There seems to be a pair of entry holes in the exterior housing of their primary drive engine. The rim of the entry holes is visibly glowing from heat!"

Ronin didn't fail to notice that Delacroix's report made LeCroy visibly excited. "Lieutenant LeCroy, it appears you like your new toy?" he asked with a broad smile.

LeCroy's enthusiastic reply brought smiles to everyone's faces. Nodding emphatically, he said, "Oh YESSIR! I believe we might like having another big horse in our stable." Turning serious, LeCroy added, "Our other weapons systems are ready to fire. We're rapidly approaching the enemy ship now that it's no longer accelerating. What do you want me to do, Captain?"

Ronin thought about it for a moment. "Permanently disable their engines with a few more shots, and destroy any of their boarding pods we might find so they can't try to board Cerberus. When we're done with that, let's tow the enemy ship back towards Sanctuary."

"Aye, Captain!"responded several of the crew. They were going to be busy for the next few hours.

CHAPTER 31

SANCTUARY

"**A**ny way to sneak past them?" Gozen asked over their commlink.

Gonzales didn't think so. "Negative. Tangos seem to be using the entrance to that wing as some sort of command post."

Gozen and Gonzales were crouched on top of a heavy duty utility pipe, their liquid black exosuits nearly invisible in the gloomy, poorly lit area several stories above the main deck of Sanctuary's central hub. Both Marines continued to watch the video feed displayed on their visors, which was transmitted from their sole remaining Butterfly drone. They were searching for a way in.

"Naturally the protocol officer is hiding up in that wing somewhere. I suppose we can't just walk down the hull on the outside?" Gonzales asked.

Gozen shook his head. "If only. Sanctuary has some sort of anti-intruder system active on the outside hull. We go out there while there's still hostiles lurking about, we ain't coming back." He panned the camera around when his eyes saw something he liked. "See those light panel towers on both sides of the entrance?"

Gonzales nodded. The entrance to the wing was lit by a pair of "towers" of lights that vertically ran up the length of the edge of the entrance, so they were highly visible against the dimmer, metallic-colored interior of Sanctuary.

Gozen continued. "Several paces to the outside of those towers are power banks. We knock those out, plunge this sector into darkness, and scoot past the hostiles milling about on the deck before they get themselves sorted out."

Nodding more enthusiastically now, Gonzales snorted. "I like it. Simple. Easy to remember. We're in range with my mag-rail and your buzzsaw."

"I've got a better idea," said Gozen. "Let our Butterfly do the work for us. Bring it back and use it to place some boomsticks on the power banks. Much quieter."

Gonzales couldn't help but laugh. "The Sanctuary folks aren't going to be too happy with you blowing everything up inside the station."

"They can add it to my tab," Gozen retorted with a smile.

Butterfly drones can carry a pound of cargo, so Gonzales attached a single stick when it arrived. The top of each power bank was wide enough for the drone to set the stick down without it rolling off. He brought the drone back and repeated the procedure for the other power bank.

When the drone had returned, he stowed it by reattaching it to his suit. Gonzales had long ago stopped thinking about the incongruous picture that a device which resembled an actual butterfly painted when it is attached to a lethal looking exosuit. Then Gonzales looked at Gozen. "Charges set," he said.

"It's Go Time," replied Gozen, two seconds before he remotely triggered the charges and detonated the boomsticks. The powerful, simultaneous explosions rocked the entrance to the wing and the surrounding interior area of Sanctuary. Lights quickly went out, but not before Gozen saw a fair bit of smoke gush forth and obscure the entrance. "Not bad, it's dark AND smoky. Let's shove off!" Gozen continued.

They moved down to the deck and towards the entrance. The smoke wasn't thick enough to obscure the starlight image on their visors, which clearly showed their path through the chaos and mob milling around.

"Keep dodging those Ullrians!" Gozen said. Some of the Ullrians were drifting towards the Marines, who were silently sneaking among them. Just as he spoke, a few Ullrians activated torchlights, but their weak light was lost in the cavernous entrance and served only to create a few shadows.

"Oh, geez! Am I glad our exosuits are hard to see!" muttered Gonzalez to himself as they continued weaving between moving obstacles.

In the lead now, Gozen led them to the darkest wall of the wing entrance that was furthest from the torch lights. It was also the wall with the fewest Ullrians, as they had started migrating towards the lights. Gozen found a dark niche in the wall that turned out to be a hatchway to a room with some crates stacked outside. It was the perfect place to hide while they waited a minute for more Ullrians to move to the lights.

"Perfect! They've abandoned this side. Let's move further up the wing before they bring in more lights. Tacnet is showing fewer Ullrians that way," Gozen said over their commlink as he exited their temporary hide.

The two scrambled much faster now that they didn't have to bob and weave their way past blinded Ullrians. That only lasted until they reached their next obstacle, more light. They had reached the next section of the wing where the lights still functioned.

Gozen and Gonzales took cover in another hatchway that was still deeply shadowed, while Gozen peeked around the edge to take a long visual of the wing.

Gonzales' voice seemed subdued on the commlink. "Tacnet says it's pretty quiet in this neighborhood. There's no one showing up on my plot except Greene."

"Yeah, I don't see anyone with my Mark I's either," Gozen replied, referring to his eyeballs as he continued looking. "Looks like everyone in this section was captured by the Ullrians and taken aboard their ship before it moved away."

"Where's our guy now?" Gonzales asked, mostly rhetorically since they could both see his location on their Tacnet displays.

"Stationary. Still over by that fire suppression system," Gozen noted.

It was Gonzales' turn to take a look, so they switched places and Gonzales did a slow visual scan.

"I see some unused escape pods next to the fire suppression system, and some sort of station machinery beyond that. There's not much for us to hide behind if this goes down the wrong way. The lighting in this section is too far away for us to take out, too. I'm not a fan of this situation, Echo 8."

Gonzales cranked the optics power on his visor up to look more closely at the area where Greene should be. "I see ... not much, really. How's this guy supposed to hide in that? All I see is a tangled-up hose behind that housing, some buttons, and a spinner to roll up the hose."

Gozen took a chance and leaned out past Gonzales, exposing himself more than he should have. As he did so, he likewise cranked up his visor optics.

Gozen grunted as he looked over the area. "Where IS this guy?" he muttered as he slowly checked out the area.

A small movement of the tangled fire hose suddenly caught Gozen's attention and he riveted his eyes to that spot. "Echo 6. He's not near the fire suppression system, he's IN the fire suppression system!" Gozen stated.

"Well, well, well. Let's get him outta here before that mob of Ullrians we left gets themselves organized," Gonzales said.

"Right. This area won't stay empty for long. Let's move!" Gozen ordered. They left their hide and broke into a trot. It didn't take long to cover the distance to their objective.

While Gozen knelt down to look into the fire suppression system and get Greene's attention, Gonzales kept his eyes peeled for any sign they'd been seen.

A high-pitched shriek startled Gonzales and for a moment he thought a child was dying a painful death. He turned to look at its source, and saw the sound came from Leroy Greene.

"Shut up already, Greene!" growled Gozen over his external speaker.

Somehow, Greene emitted an even higher pitched wail, his face a rictus of fear as he cowered behind the fire hose and tried to become one with the interior back wall of the fire suppression system.

"Greene! We're Marines from Cerberus. Snap out of it or we won't be able to rescue you!" snarled Gonzales through his own suit's external speaker. Just then, Gozen was able to grab Greene's ankle, and he began to drag him out of his hiding spot.

While Greene shrieked even louder, Gozen stood him up and smacked him upside the head to get his attention. It worked. "Stop cry-ing like a little girl and listen up, Mr. Greene. You don't cooperate, we might not be able to bring you back to Cerberus. Understand?" Gozen nearly growled.

Greene nodded meekly, his tear-filled eyes informing the Marines that he had barely regained some sort of control over his terror. Greene turned to show Gonzales his bloody shoulder.

"Echo 8, Green is wounded and bleeding badly. I'm going to apply an ouch pouch to stop the flow." Gonzales was taking out his medical kit as he spoke.

"Copy that. But make it quick, Tacnet says trouble is definitely headed our way now.

Before Gonzales could say another word, a chorus of wild howls came from the darkened area down the wing. Gozen turned to look in that direction while Gonzales continued to apply medical aid to Greene. Their exosuit audio feeds picked up the sound of running feet.

"Greene's shrieking just attracted every Ullrian within earshot, Echo 6," Gozen noted dryly as he checked his ammunition levels on Tacnet. They were running low and Tacnet showed hundreds of Ullrians scrambling their way.

Gonzales just nodded as he finished the patch on Greene, and he stood to join Gozen. They prepared to defend themselves from a tidal wave of angry savages.

CHAPTER 32

SOLARA

"**C**aptain? We've received the latest update from Echo 8. They're extremely low on ammunition and fully engaged by a horde of Ullrians. Tacnet data indicates they're outnumbered fifty to one," reported LeCroy.

"How soon until Bulldog 1 arrives with Gamma team?" Ronin asked.

"Ten minutes," LeCroy said.

Sitting in his Captain's chair, Ronin pursed his lips in frustration. His people just didn't have that much time or ammunition remaining.

Mueller was standing next to Ronin and leaned towards him slightly. "That doesn't factor in the time it'll take to make their way inside Sanctuary to reach them, either," she murmured.

Ronin knew that. He also knew his Marines could escape using their exosuits if they weren't tied down protecting Leroy Greene.

LeCroy interrupted his thoughts. "Tacnet update coming in. Echo 6 and 8 are out of ammunition. The area is saturated with multiple fires from various explosions, and there are numerous dead and wounded Ullrians all over."

At least they're making a good account of themselves while they can, Ronin thought. *Meanwhile, we're stuck out here collecting that ship we shot up. Or zapped. Or pulsed? Need to settle on some terminology when using our swanky new ray gun.*

The electronic sound that began emanating from Delacroix's station barely caught anyone's attention.

"Multiple escape pod launches from Sanctuary." Delacroix noted to no one in particular, not bothering to identify the number of pods launching for everyone this time. There had been dozens of pod launches in the past few hours.

LeCroy's next statement had the opposite effect. "Echo 8 and 6 have abandoned the station in an escape pod. They took Mr. Greene along for the ride!"

"Can you identify which pod?" Mueller asked.

LeCroy shook his head. "Negative. It's one of 10 that launched. They're all headed down to the planetary surface at high speed. Predicted landing coordinates are widely dispersed."

"Redirect Bulldog 1 to intercept the most likely pod and retrieve them if possible," Ronin ordered.

"Do we want to pull in one of the other Bulldogs from the operation to capture the enemy ship?" Mueller asked. The other four Bulldogs were engaged in the efforts to take over the ship they had disabled.

"Negative. We can't allow them time to repair the ship and threaten Sanctuary or Cerberus," Ronin responded in a tone of voice that clearly said he'd prefer to send ALL the Bulldogs to hunt down the escape pod.

The next few hours were going to pass slowly.

***

"Whoaaaaaaa!" groaned Gonzalez after he had triggered the escape pod's emergency launch system and the pod blasted away from Sanctuary. The powerful acceleration in the pod threatened to crush them into mush and left the three of them unable to breathe for long periods of time. Almost too long. Clearly the acceleration had been tuned with 1.5G Solarans in mind instead of 1.0G humans from Earth.

Finally it eased off and they were left weightless inside the tiny craft. They had barely had enough time to get strapped in before their hasty departure. Gozen hadn't even had time to unseal his exosuit helmet. As Gozen's hands began to move upwards, he noticed Gonzales put his helmet back on.

The commlink that opened between them carried a warning. "Echo 8, I recommend we stay buttoned up," Gonzales said.

Gozen's eyebrows shot up inside his suit. "Affirmative, Echo 6. Is there an air leak in the cabin?" Gozen was worried whether Greene would have enough air to survive the trip down to the planet's surface.

Gonzales snorted. "That's a negative. We should be so lucky. The air is fouled."

Foul air? Gozen wondered. He was immediately alarmed even though there didn't appear to be any smoke evident in the cabin. "We need to secure breathable air for Mr. Greene," he ordered.

Gonzales shook his head. "Negative on that, Echo 8. Mr. Greene is WHY the air is fouled." With that, Gonzales motioned towards Leroy Greene with a slight head nod.

Inside his exosuit helmet, Gozen's unseen eyes slowly looked towards Greene and he beheld the horror.

Gozen couldn't help himself. "Ooooh. Oh. Aw man!" he exclaimed, his voice growing higher pitched with each word and ending in a revolted, disgusted tone.

"For the record, Echo 8, the nickname "Cap'n Ray Gun" was already given to a POW we took on the Terra Station mission," Gonzales noted dryly.

"Yeah, but that was just a reference to his weapon because we hadn't encountered those before."

Gozen was checking the craft's simple interface as he replied. "Twenty minutes until we're on the ground. We're landing on the far northern part of the central ... island, I'd guess you'd call it. Looks more like a big island with land bridges leading to each of the other large islands. Our intel briefing says they're "continents" controlled by various Factions. And on a hot world like Solara, this central island actually means jungle."

Gonzales was silent for a few moments. "Ullrians," he stated simply.

Nodding, Gozen didn't need to elaborate. Their intel briefing also noted that the northernmost landmass was the homeland of the Ullrians. They would be landing closest to that fun bunch.

"The *Deuce* is gonna love seeing more Ullrians," Gonzales finally said over the commlink, again nodding slightly towards a very miserable Leroy Greene curled up in his seat. Greene had pulled his knees towards his chest like a child does.

Nodding now, Gozen agreed with both the statement and the new nickname, although he refined it a bit to fit the owner's snobbish attitude. "That's *Mister Deuce* to you. Now we wait."

CHAPTER 33

BOOTS ON THE GROUND

The small escape pod landed with surprising gentleness in a small jungle clearing. Because they were designed to quickly whisk away possibly injured occupants from a highly dangerous situation, the pods featured the Solaran's powerful sublight drives and automated flight systems. They also carried very small caches of medical and food supplies, as the pods were only intended to be used to land on a planet's surface where help would be nearby.

"How is it we managed to land in the only jungle on a mostly desert-like planet?" muttered Gonzales as he lowered the ramp of the pod. He had removed his helmet to get some fresh air now that they were on the surface. Extreme heat and humidity quickly flooded the pod cabin and filled his nostrils with unfamiliar, cloying vegetative scents as he stomped down the ramp.

A helmetless Gozen joined him at the bottom. "Solara is roughly 70% ocean, and 25% arid terrain, and somehow this infernal machine chose to land us in the only jungle on the planet?"

Gonzales shook his head. "It's even more nuts that we're in the cooler, nearly polar region of the planet and it's STILL this hot and humid. Only some of the land is cool enough to be occupied by humans. Land that isn't too far south."

"Those, and where the Ullrians are up north at the mountainous arctic region, are relatively frigid in parts. Crazy planet," Gozen remarked.

They heard a grunt and groan behind them and turned to look. Leroy Greene was slowly walking down the ramp. He carefully placed each foot and tested the grip before moving on to the next step down the ramp. His wounded shoulder remained securely wrapped by the ouch pouch Gonzales applied back on Sanctuary.

"Looks like 1.5Gs don't agree with Mr. Deuce," Gozen said, speaking quietly so Greene wouldn't overhear.

"I don't think he finds too much that's agreeable to his delicate sensibilities on this whole mission. He has poor physical fitness, poor people skills, and he's weak," Gonzalez replied with a snort in a similarly quiet tone.

"Yes, but he grew up in the 'right' sort of neighborhood and attended only the best schools. Just ask him. He'll tell you."

Gozen raised his right pinky to signify hoity toity-ness. "You know the drill. We're just the hired help, and we don't know nothing," Gozen stated, adopting a guttural sounding accent for his quiet quip.

Turning businesslike, he continued in a normal tone of voice. "We don't know how long we'll be stuck here on our own. Could be a few hours due to the number of pods that were launched at the same time. In the meantime, we need to establish a defensive perimeter as best we can. We stay in our exosuits to keep us more mobile and take turns looking for trouble. We're going to have to make do without additional drones or other early warning gear."

Nodding, Gonzales volunteered. "I'll take first shift and do a sweep around and map it to Tacnet. Go out say, 500 yards?"

"Yeah. That's a good distance for the initial survey. Make a note of potential water sources if you stumble across any. Mr. Deuce doesn't have an exosuit, so he'll become pretty thirsty unless we can find some water to filter clean for him."

"Well, we can't allow any discomfort, can we? I'll tell the maids to turn down the pillows for him before we tuck him in for a nap, too," Gonzales noted as he put his helmet back on so he could run the survey as much as he did just to escape the heat and humidity. He stepped away and used his exosuit's power to quickly bound away before Greene made it down to the bottom of the ramp.

"Where are we supposed to stay down here?" Greene asked when he reached Gozen, puffing heavily as he arrived.

"Accommodations not up to your expectations, Mr. Greene?" Gozen said in an even tone and a cocked eyebrow.

Not picking up on Gozen's sarcasm, Greene plowed ahead. "Why couldn't you have set us down in a civilized area, for Heaven's sake?"

Keeping his irritation held in an iron grip now, Gozen managed to keep his tone steady. "I'll be sure to pass along your objections about fully autopiloted escape pods to the customer service department."

Turning away from Greene, Gozen took another long look at their surroundings while Greene processed Gozen's words. Greene wasn't bright enough to realize these escape pods were designed to safely land people who aren't pilots, or who may be too injured to manually fly anything themselves, and to get them to the surface quickly in the assumption that surface rescue would never be far away.

Sudden movement caught Gozen's eyes as a human burst from the jungle tree line about 300 yards away at the edge of the clearing they occupied. The unidentified person sprinted towards their position past clumps of grass waving in the clearing.

"To arms! Get back inside Mr. Greene!" yelled Gozen as he slammed his helmet back on. Gozen immediately could hear Gonzales' voice over a commlink.

"Echo 8, Echo 6. Multiple inbound bogies, your position, on Tacnet."

Gozen noticed the strain in Gonzales' voice from moving quickly in the heavy gravity, and Tacnet also showed Gonzales rapidly returning to the pod from deep into the jungle, in addition to the bogies.

As Greene shuffled back up the pod ramp, Gozen reached back and pulled a captured Monosabre from where he had attached it to his exosuit. He had run out of ammunition for everything except the Firefly he brought along before they departed Sanctuary and appropriated the Monosabre of an Ullrian who Gozen had ensured wouldn't be needing it any longer.

The person sprinting to him was moving fast. Too fast. As he approached, Gozen made out additional details. It was a young Ullrian man, and he was running for all he was worth. Gozen's external microphones also picked up something he hadn't expected to hear.

"Waaaaaahhh!!!" the young man yelled. It obviously wasn't a war cry, it was the sound of someone running for his life towards the only possible safety that he could. Right at the escape pod.

Additional movement at the tree line drew Gozen's eyes. Two gigantic tiger-like felines bounded out of the trees in hot pursuit of the Ullrian.

Gozen's eyes grew wide at the sight. "Echo 6, Echo 8. Be advised, we have a young Ullrian fleeing towards our position. What's your ETA?"

"Echo 8, twenty seconds ... Fleeing what?" Gonzales asked.

"Looks like a mutant pair of oversized Bengal tigers," Gozen said as Greene finally hobbled back inside the pod. Gozen ran up the ramp after him and spun the wheel in the center of the door hatch to seal it closed using his free hand. While he finished sealing the hatch, Gozen's eyes scanned Tacnet, and he couldn't believe how much ground both the Ullrian and the mutant cats covered in just a few seconds. Gonzales was not going to make it back before the party arrived.

Gozen resumed his position at the bottom of the ramp and he made ready to take out the young Ullrian. Seconds later, Gozen was greatly surprised when the young man arrived and skidded to a stop. With a sardonic salute towards Gozen to acknowledge his presence, the young man drew his own Monosabre and he spun around to face the onrushing mutant tigers.

Gozen was very confused as he reported the unexpected development to Gonzalez. "Echo 6 be advised, the Ullrian has taken up a defensive position next to me."

"I hope you know how to use that thing, because we're about to become cat food if you don't," the Ullrian said with a tilt of his head towards the tigers. Seeing their prey had turned to face them and was standing next to another human, the tigers had likewise slowed their approach.

Just then, Gonzalez arrived and joined the two facing the oncoming tigers. "That's like twice the size of a freaking tiger!" he exclaimed over the commlink and his external speakers at the same time. As he said so, he raised the makeshift weapon he had acquired in the Jungle because he, too, was out of ammunition. It was a tree branch that he had torn from the trunk of a tree using the power of his exosuit.

It was the Ullrian's turn to look confused and he shot the Marines a glance. "A tiger from … the old Earth legends? Where have you been? These are Hellcats. Everybody knows that."

By now, the Hellcats had arrived, stopping about 10 yards away. They paced back and forth in place to assess the new scenario. They were truly frightening.

The external microphones of the Marines' exosuits picked up the impossibly deep, bass growling of the Hellcats. Gozen swore he could feel the ground rumbling even through his exosuit.

Gozen's blood ran cold when the growling suddenly formed words.

"Humaaaaans," one of the giant Hellcats said in its gravelly voice. "Diiiieeeee."

"Echo 8 … did the giant kitty just freakin' SPEAK??" yelled Gonzales over the commlink and external speakers. Panic colored his words.

"Oh, man, that just ain't right!" Gozen yelled back as he brandished his Monosabre and moved to stand between Gonzalez and the Ullrian while the tigers continued to pace and shake the earth with angry roars. Gozen and the Ullrian traded a brief glance and Gozen couldn't help but see the mixture of fear and determination on the young man's face.

"If we die today, we die as friends and comrades, with honor and glory," the Ullrian said to them, before returning his gaze to the feline threats. Gozen and Gonzales simply nodded in return.

With a sudden snarl, the cats attacked as one with blinding speed. They had chosen to attack the person in the middle. Gozen.

The Ullrian and Gonzales leaped away, one to each side of the attacking cats. They both hacked at the felines with their weapons, while Gozen decided to rely on the protection of his exosuit armor and met them head on.

The Ullrian missed with his Monosabre as the nearest giant tiger nimbly avoided the weapon. Gonzales managed to inflict a powerful blow with his makeshift club on the other one. It just didn't seem to have any effect.

Gozen slashed downwards with his Monosabre and managed to draw blood just before a swipe of a giant paw hit him anyway. The Hellcat's blow was so powerful that Gozen was swatted aside and sent sprawling 10 yards away.

One of the Hellcats moved to pounce on Gozen, but the young Ullrian, who positioned himself between the Hellcat and the stunned Marine, intercepted it. Gonzales sprang over to join the Ullrian, waiving his makeshift club menacingly. Both tigers regrouped and attacked single file. Standing side-by-side, the Ullrian and Gonzales braced themselves for the impact.

From somewhere behind Gonzales and the Ullrian youth, a streak of blue fire hurtled towards the Hellcats. It moved too fast to actually see, although it left an observer with the faint impression of having seen the strike of a powerful lightning bolt from an angry deity. The angry shriek of its fiery passage trailed behind.

By the time the Ullrian and Gonzales reacted, the streak was long gone. It had passed through the lead Hellcat, nicked the trailing Hellcat, and tore into the Jungle several hundred yards away. It was hard to determine who was more surprised, the Ullrian, Gonzales, or the wounded Hellcat who was knocked aside only to discover it was missing part of its front shoulder.

The wounded Hellcat roared in a terrifying mixture of hate, anger, pain, and blood lust as it tried to regain its footing. Gozen sprang forward to attack while it was more vulnerable, yelling "Get some!" over the commlink and his external speakers.

The Ullrian and Gonzales wasted no time joining Gozen in the attack. They quickly surrounded the badly wounded Hellcat, and each time it attempted to attack one of its tormentors, another one would take a stab at it. The terrible wound prevented it from escaping, and the three humans quickly vanquished the monstrous Hellcat with Monosabre stabs, slashes, and good old-fashioned club bashing. All three men were left panting for breath after killing the last Hellcat. Gonzales' exosuit also was scratched up by the Hellcat.

Using only on the commlink so the Ullrian couldn't hear, Gonzales finally spoke, drawling out the words in an exaggerated Texas accent. "Nice shootin'. I can't believe you used a Firefly to kill cute little kittens, Gung Ho."

Snorting, Gozen muttered, "Cute little kitties my hairy behind. Right tools, right job." It was an old saying in the Marines.

Gonzales tilted his chin towards the tube that Gozen was reattaching to the back of his exosuit. "That the prototype Mark II Firefly? I couldn't help but notice you didn't have to pick yourself up off the ground after firing it."

"That's affirmative. Lieutenant Alphonso swore it uses a small gravity compensator based on some of the tech we acquired during the engagement with Warspite. It reduced the recoil just enough to stop kicking us down when firing. Barely. Still feels like a mule kick though," Gozen said, looking down at his exosuit where the Hellcat had swiped him. There were four long scratches faintly gouging the extremely tough, inky black suit material. "Looks like the new upgrades to our suits to resist Monosabres also works for Hellcats, too," he added.

"Nice of Lt. Alphonso to provide us with the upgrade, then." Gonzales said appreciatively.

Gozen snorted. "Lt. Gustav tactically acquired them somehow. He refused to say exactly how."

Inside their exosuits, Tacnet suddenly began showing the approach of a dozen humans. They were moving rapidly and approaching the tree line of the clearing that was several hundred yards distant.

Both Marines turned to look, taking cover as they did so and pulling the confused young Ullrian down to hide with them. A small party of Ullrians appeared, and Gozen groaned inside his exosuit. He was already badly bruised from the last twenty minutes of combat.

The young Ullrian stood up and waved at the approaching group. They were making a beeline for the escape pod anyway, so they really didn't change direction much.

By the time the group of Ullrians arrived, both Gozen and Gonzales were standing next to the young Ullrian. There wasn't any point in hiding after the kid began waving.

The group's leader was an Ullrian with leathery skin that bore the scars of many battles. He had a shield and battleaxes that all appeared to use Monosabre technology in their blades. His face was impassive and seemed carved from granite as he pulled his battleaxes from their sheaths on his back. Looking first at the remains of two Hellcats, then at the young Ullrian, the man finally spoke as the remaining Ullrians likewise unsheathed their weapons.

"Sojourner, explain yourself," the man said simply. His deep, gravelly voice almost seemed inhuman. His pale blue eyes shone piercingly in the light of the clearing, and his braided blonde hair was streaked with gray. The braiding served to keep the hair out of the man's eyes during combat.

The young Ullrian traded glances with the Marines in their inky black exosuits, noting they were preparing to defend themselves against the newcomers. "Father, these two warriors and I defended ourselves as allies against two Hellcats."

Eyebrows furrowing, the man seemed perplexed. "TWO Hellcats?" he asked, knowing the large felines typically hunted alone. The presence of the otherworldly looking allies his son had joined wasn't helping clarify the situation for him. He could also hear the murmurs of confusion behind him among the Ullrians at this news.

The kid nodded. "Yes, father. Two. I was being chased by the first Hellcat and saw this escape pod land here, so I ran to it and encountered these two. They bravely fought with great skill, and saved my life. We three will share the teeth. I name them 'Friends of Ullr.'"

The leader's eyebrows shot up at his son's statement about sharing the teeth and naming them Friends of Ullr. He glanced at the Ullrians surrounding him and nodded slightly. They put away their weapons.

Inside their exosuits, Gonzales commlinked Gozen. "Echo 8, what is happening here?"

"I think we just passed some sort of test, or initiation rite, or something. Follow along," Gozen ordered.

"Then your Sojourney has been more successful than any before you," the Ullrian leader said to his son, before gesturing to the Marines. "Come, friends. We have much celebrating to do. Wine to drink, stories to share, and feasting awaits us back in Ullr. Will you join us?"

Nodding and speaking over the external speakers for the first time since the party of Ullrians arrived, Gozen said, "It would be our great honor to join our friends in celebration."

Over the commlink, Gonzales couldn't help himself. "Geez, could you have possibly sounded any cheesier just then?"

Gozen snorted, glad the Ullrians couldn't hear exosuit commlinks. "If sounding cheesy avoids another tough fight and scores a party for us, I'm all in. Let's collect those teeth, and update Green with our new situation and leave a report for the LT. Green will remain with the pod, and we'll go with our new friends."

As he said this over commlink, the Ullrian leader approached and shook hands with each of the Marines. "I am Leif Galruud. Chieftain of the Ullr. You have met my son, Seth, already." He turned and motioned for the other Ullrians to join them, and continued making introductions between the new friends.

Soon the Marines and Seth were adorned with 3-inch long teeth of the Hellcats around their necks, which the Ullrians had bestowed on them a surprising amount of seriousness and ceremony. The Marines learned they would travel to Ullr on the small aircraft the Ullrians had parked about 10 miles from their current position. They only had to hike through the Jungle on a 1.5 G world first.

I sure hope I'm right about this, Gozen thought to himself. Leaving Greene without adult supervision while they joined the Ullrians was a calculated risk that Gozen hoped would pay off.

CHAPTER 34

CERBERUS

"**C**aptain, the Gamma team boarding party reports the light resistance has been mopped up and the surviving Ullrian crew taken into custody. After the enemy ship lost power, it got extremely cold inside the hull and oxygen levels dropped dangerously low," reported LeCroy.

Ronin's collar commlink suddenly chimed, and he thumbed it open. "Ronin here."

Chief Medical Officer Hirohito Takema's voice was loud and clear over the commlink. "Captain, you wanted an update from Sickbay? We are treating several hundred cases of severe hypothermia, hypoxemia and frostbite. Most of the prisoners were very close to being 'corpsicles' when Gamma boarded their ship. We also have a few dozen burn unit cases and radiological contamination to treat. Whatever you used to hit that ship really blasted a lot of energy into it."

Ronin couldn't help but nod to himself as he replied. "Thank you, Doctor. Marine casualties?"

"Just some light wear and tear with bumps and bruises. They've been treated and released back into the wild already," Taketa noted.

"Alright. Keep the Bridge advised if the situation changes down there. Ronin out."

Mueller and Ronin traded glances as they stood near the tactical station on the Bridge. Mueller spoke first. "We're going to need to develop a medical approach towards casualties from energy weapons."

Ronin just nodded, his gray eyes hardening as he did so. "Agreed. I've also been jotting down some notes about this new reality and passed them along to the search and rescue crew chiefs already. I asked them to review our procedures for rescue of injured persons from power sources like fires or electrical burns, and pass them along to Dr. Taketa. He's already been read into the need to buff and polish our processes and develop new ones because of our new weapon system."

Mueller's left eyebrow raised sharply. "I didn't even see you did that already."

Ronin snorted softly. "Sent them some quick text messages, and all confirmed receipt. Taketa will be a pioneer in the field of emergency medicine for treatment of wounds from energy weapons."

Mueller shook her head ruefully. "New types of weapons. Treatments for the wounds inflicted by them. It makes me wonder whether adding new weapons is worth it sometimes."

Ronin nodded thoughtfully. "Yes. What we know of our species' history is filled with the race between weapons advancement, followed by new medical treatments for the injuries the new weapons can inflict. Sometimes medicine wins. Sometimes it doesn't."

LeCroy, who was seated at the tactical station, and Mueller, who was standing next to him, both looked at Ronin. He was alluding to The Fall, at least partially.

Ronin decided to explain a bit further. "When The Fall happened, mankind had to rely upon natural immunity and survival of the fittest to endure, because medicine never had a chance to catch up to the sweeping plague that was released. But I've been studying ancient records of our lost history from before The Fall that the Ark brought to Terra Station. There were many military advances in weaponry and tactics, and most, if given enough time, were eventually followed by medical advances.

"In the days of bladed weapons, we developed treatments for slashing and stab wounds. As warfare evolved, better treatments were devised for projectile weapons and diseases encountered on the battlefields, and so on. War has always brought death and tragedy, but it has also spurred the development of life-saving treatments for injuries, chronic conditions and other ailments."

LeCroy looked somewhat perplexed. "So, Dr. Taketa's developments will just be another chapter in a story that ... takes us where?"

Mueller raised an eyebrow as she traded glances with LeCroy before she answered that question. "The future, Lieutenant LeCroy, the future."

Ronin's commlink node chimed with another incoming message.

"Captain Ronin? This is Lieutenant Sunderland. Bulldog 1 has located the escape pod Echo 6 and 8 used to rescue Greene, and they have retrieved Green. Our Marines were no longer with him. They encountered a party of Ullrians on the surface and are attached to them."

"Attached? What does THAT mean?" Ronin asked. Upon hearing the word "Ullrians," Ronin immediately feared for the safety of his Marines, but the modifier "attached," instead of "killed" or "captured," wasn't among the possible outcomes he might have anticipated.

Sunderland's voice clearly communicated his own lack of certainty about the situation. "Greene reports our Marines voluntarily accompanied the Ullrians back to their home continent as some sort of formalized friendship process. Echo 8 requests we get drones overhead to re-establish commlink contact. He's hoping we can leverage this opportunity to establish a relationship with the Ullrians."

Ronin nodded thoughtfully. "Agreed. Have Bulldog 1 return to Cerberus. Meanwhile, I want you to fit out a Bulldog to jump into the atmosphere and seed the drone network over the Ullr continent to make this happen. Ronin out."

Ronin's gray eyes settled on Delgado for a moment. "Lieutenant, notify Dr. Wright of the situation. Advise him I want to see his ideas for establishing a relationship with the Ullrians. He should continue his work on how we can do the same for each of the other Factions without getting any more of our people killed. We'll meet tomorrow at 0800 hours in the main conference room to discuss."

"Aye, Captain." responded Delgado before she turned back to her instruments to pass along the orders.

Mueller looked at Ronin for a second. "Have the remaining Factions decided whether they're agreeable to a worldwide meeting of their leadership? What did they call it? A council or something?"

Ronin corrected her. "When I last spoke with the bosses from the Cosa Nostra and the Zulu, both called it a 'Continental Congress.' They pointed out that a Continental Congress hadn't taken place in over 200 years because of all the fighting and mistrust between the Factions, plus an assassination of a key Faction leader that occurred at the final Congress held. The arrival of a ship from Earth might just change that."

Mueller looked surprised. "What?" Ronin asked.

In a voice betraying her disbelief, Mueller asked, "You mean the end of the Continental Congress wasn't a result of how Ullrians behavior? They seem to prefer killing over trusting. Or making friends. Or even just leaving anyone else alone, for that matter."

Ronin snickered softly, but Cerberus AI interrupted him before he could say a word.

"Commander Mueller, the historical records from Solara that we have now obtained strongly suggest the Ullrians did not initiate the end of the Continental Congress. The Ullrians were trying to save it, and their Faction leader, who was serving as delegate at the assembly, was assassinated by a drug cartel supported by the Cosa Nostra and a former Faction.

"The Ullrians of that day were seeking an end to the production and distribution of a highly addictive drug that was poisoning many people on all the continents. After their beloved leader was killed, the Ullrians went on the warpath and began punishing the Factions responsible for his death and for the existence of that drug. Even though the Ullrians were always fewer in number than the other Factions, their warlike existence enabled them to overcome their numerical disadvantage."

Muller's face clearly showed her shock. "The Ullrians have been extracting revenge for a killing over two centuries ago?"

The AI responded again. "Yes. Even though our acquired data shows the Ullrians eradicated that drug many decades ago, they continue their revenge campaign against the remaining Factions they believe are responsible."

LeCroy, who couldn't help eavesdropping as the conversation was still taking place at his tactical station, interrupted. "Remaining Factions? I thought there were only seven Factions?"

Ronin nodded and answered before the AI could. "The Ullrians wiped out the eighth Faction over a century ago. They were called the Camino del Sol, which translates as 'the Way of the Sun.' The assassin belonged to that Faction, so the Ullrians concentrated on destroying them first, since they were primarily responsible for both the drugs and the assassination."

Ronin stopped to clear his throat slightly before he continued. "While the Ullrians are terrifying enemies, they are also terrific allies. The two Factions who we now have learned are friendly to the Ullrians were never responsible for any of those crimes, and there has not been a single clash between them and the Ullrians in centuries.

"Captured Ullrian data supports this conclusion as well. Those three Factions are loyal in the extreme, but slow to allow a new friendship to begin due to their mistrust of outsiders. History has given those three Factions plenty of reasons to support their mistrust."

Mueller shook her head. "Dr. Wright has his work cut out for him. This planet's situation is just as messed up as Earth was during the war."

Ronin politely demurred. "I'm ... not so sure about that. In many ways, several Factions have remained remarkably consistent in their allies and relations between them for centuries. We've ascertained there are now only two unpredictable Factions still remaining—Zulu and Cosa Nostra."

It was Mueller's turn to look surprised. "The same two Factions we've been dealing with the most?"

Ronin nodded. "The same. Dr. Wright and I have been discussing why those Factions seemed so agreeable to our arrival. We've jointly concluded they hope to gain strategic advantages over the other Factions by allying with us before the others, and by demanding we ally with them exclusively. Once they realize that isn't how the Confederacy will want to play the game, chances are high one or both Factions will turn openly hostile and engage in dangerous actions to prevent us from establishing relationships with any other Faction."

LeCroy blew out a breath of air. "So our goal is to establish relationships with all of them?" he asked.

"Preferably. Hopefully," Ronin stated. "Ideally they would finally form a planetary government the Confederacy can open relations with. Otherwise, we may just end up playing one Faction off the other and build the alliance we can trust the most. That's why we're reaching out to all the Factions using the contact information Sanctuary gave us.

"Sanctuary isn't a Faction, but they're hoping we can help establish a peaceful, planet-wide government since it's in most everyone's best interest. The problem is not everyone will want to understand that a peaceful union is in their best interests. Cerberus will be asking each Faction to agree to a Continental Congress."

Both LeCroy and Mueller nodded now. Convincing some of the competing Factions to give up short-term gain for themselves in favor of long-term gain that helps everyone might be a tough sell.

CHAPTER 35

CEASE FIRE

"So, the Ullrians agreed to the return of their people even though we took them prisoner in their raid on Sanctuary? Just like that?" Lieutenant Gustav's voice couldn't sound more incredulous as he questioned Dr. Wright.

Cerberus' officers were gathered in the main conference room for Dr. Wright's presentation several days after Gonzales and Gozen traveled to Ullr. The lights were dimmed for the holo briefing.

Wright froze the holo in the center of the main table for a moment. Acknowledging Gustav with a nod, he responded, "That is correct, Lieutenant Gustav. Ullrians typically don't surrender. However, the batch you took into custody was essentially incapacitated and unable to defend themselves.

"According to the Ullrian creed, these warriors never surrendered. They didn't voluntarily give themselves up. Accordingly, they never lost their honor, and so they may return to their Faction.

"Thanks to the two Marines who accepted the Ullrians' invitation to visit their home continent, Cerberus has an established a line of communication with their Faction leadership through a drone network that's been seeded over the planet. They've agreed to a cease-fire, ordered their prisoners aboard our ship to behave in exchange for their return, and will send delegates to a Continental Congress."

This was too much for Gustav to believe. "What's to stop the Ullrians from reneging and attacking Cerberus like they attacked Sanctuary?"

Ronin answered this question. "Because they've pledged on their Faction's honor. Turns out the Ullrians have never made an actual agreement with Sanctuary. In the Ullrian's eyes, Sanctuary was always fair game because Sanctuary would also provide aid to the Zulu and Cosa Nostra.

"Once the Ullrians make a pledge on their honor, there are no known instances where they haven't fulfilled that pledge. Even the records we hacked from the Zulu and Cosa Nostra databanks support that conclusion. If it's an Ullrian pledge, they'll follow through with it or die trying rather than face dishonor."

Gustav's slowly nodded his reluctant acceptance. "Death before dishonor. Alright. I like it. That's a creed I can understand."

Dr. Wright continued with his holo presentation. "Moving on, now that we've covered the history of each population group. After some intense negotiations and creative threats or outright bribes, all seven Factions of Solara have agreed to send representatives to a Continental Congress to be held next week at a neutral site ..."

Looking highly concerned, Gustav interrupted again. "Excuse me, Dr. Wright, what neutral site? I thought Sanctuary was a legitimate target in the eyes of the Ullrians."

Dr. Wright cleared his throat. He turned to Gustav with a look of reproach, and this time replied to him as though he were addressing a misbehaving student speaking out of turn. "I'm getting to that, Lieutenant. The only neutral site agreed upon by all Factions is aboard Cerberus itself. We represent the Confederacy, and the Captain has made it clear to all during our communications with the Factions that this ship represents the only truly neutral power currently in the Solaran system."

Ronin interjected a comment now. "I've made it clear this ship intends to stay neutral, and that the Factions should be aware that we will never hesitate to defend Cerberus if attacked. If we're attacked under a false flag used as a means to get Cerberus to wrongly attack an innocent Faction, the consequences will be severe. To that end, our Marines will provide security for the Continental Congress."

Now Gustav looked decidedly unhappy. "Captain, we're combat Marines. Warding against assassination attempts requires a skill set that really isn't in our wheelhouse."

Ronin was prepared for Gustav's objections. "Understood, but we're moving forward anyway. We have little choice. Draw upon any resources you think you'll need to make it happen and get your tentative security plan to Commander Mueller and me for review."

Gustav nodded, but had to push the envelope a bit. "Would those resources happen to include the ship's AI, Captain? I may have some data probabilities and numbers and stuff that need crunching."

The faces around the table looked doubtful. Marines didn't typically interact with the Cerberus AI. None of them could recall hearing a Marine utter blasphemous (for Marines, anyway) words like "data probabilities," and "numbers." It seemed akin to a Neanderthal asking to borrow a computer to work on some spreadsheets.

The unusual request didn't faze Ronin. "Whatever you deem is necessary, Lieutenant. But my curiosity is skyrocketing. I didn't think Marines could read, much less crunch numbers," Ronin said, in a teasing tone.

"Oh, we're just simple knuckle-draggers who enjoy grunting, eating crayons and breaking other kid's toys. But, now and then... it's big brains time. Thank you, Captain. I'll get started forthwith." Gustav didn't give any more hints about his ideas.

Ronin smiled in response. "OK. Last item is food. We were running low before arriving in this system, and our supplies have only gotten lower since then. The Ullr and the Cosa Nostra Factions have agreed to restock the ship's cupboards with food and consumables, but Sanctuary has also asked to do so.

"I'm inclined to accept Sanctuary's offer. Since they are also a neutral entity, it's less likely their food will be laced with anything unpleasant in an attempt to poison us. Thoughts?" Ronin asked.

Headed nodded in response. No one disagreed with replenishing food stocks from a grateful, but officially neutral, entity whose existence they had already saved. It was the safest option.

With that, the briefing ended.

CHAPTER 36

PROCESSING

"**T**his is an outrage!" snarled the Cosa Nostra delegate, Duke Lordano, as Bravo 2, Cpl. Ed Wilson, from South Dakota, patted him down for weapons. They were at the departure site on Solara. It was little more than an empty field with some temporary security buildings guarded solely by the Cerberus Marines. They selected the remote site because they could control the entire domain.

Before Wilson could respond, a screeching sound tore across the sky, but Wilson didn't even look up to watch the latest Tomcat fighter patrol fly overhead. Taurus squadron had been relentlessly hunting the pale blue skies all day for possible airborne threats while the delegates arrived separately and departed for Cerberus.

Bravo team was patrolling the site to provide a randomized series of mobile ground defenses. Gamma team was also manning several weapons emplacements and had otherwise hidden themselves away in various ambush sites. Their inky black exosuits weren't difficult to camouflage in the terrain.

"Our apologies, Delegate Lordano. When they agreed to Cerberus as the neutral host site, each planetary Faction also agreed to abide by any security measures that Cerberus imposes for the protection of everyone," Wilson said. His external exosuit speakers also conveyed the unspoken message, *this isn't the first time I've said this today.*

Unfazed by the intimidating visage of Wilson's exosuit, Lordano let Wilson know he was underwhelmed by Wilson's apology. "Yes, well. You people should treat delegates with the respect we deserve!" he said angrily.

"That's nice, Delegate Lordano. Now strip naked!" Wilson said, this time adding some snarl and growl to his voice, giving it a menacing tone.

"WHAT!?" Lordano roared, his brown eyes glinting dangerously. As the longtime Morelino family consigliere, Lordano was used to intimidating others. Or disappearing their corpses if lesser forms of intimidation didn't work. Lordano was also used to representing the family to the other power families of his Faction, but this was the first time in centuries that the families of the Cosa Nostra had elected anyone to represent all of them as a delegate to a Continental Congress. Lordano wasn't comfortable with the new role.

"Strip naked and step through this doorway for a decontamination shower. You will receive a fresh set of clothing at the other end," Wilson said simply.

"I will not!" Lordano said, crossing his arms over his chest defiantly.

"Then you will have to explain to your Faction exactly why you failed to comply with the rules YOUR Faction agreed to for the Continental Congress!" Wilson replied, sounding menacing again. The angry voices drew the attention of Bravo 1, Gunnery Sgt. Brett Mackey, who had been standing nearby.

Mackey's deep, gravelly voice rumbled through his exosuit's external speakers, his Alabama accent also sounding menacing because he wasn't too concerned about being polite. "Delegate Lordano, you have a choice. Do what Lance Corporal Wilson says, and you will be transported to the first ship from Earth that has visited Solara in many centuries. Do not, and we will be happy to deliver you to a place of our choosing instead."

Lordano didn't like the sound of that last option. "What do you mean, a place of your choosing? I will simply return to my Faction," he snarled.

Mackey laughed aloud, his bass voice sounding threatening despite his humor. "Delegate Lordano. The Factions only agreed to the transport of delegates *to* Cerberus and their return at the conclusion of the Continental Congress. None specified what we should do with delegates who failed to follow directions and never made it to Cerberus to begin with.

"I should imagine your Faction wouldn't be pleased if you sat this one out and failed to look after its interests. Not to mention, it would be awkward wandering through the Jungle naked."

Mackey had taken to referring to the Solaran Jungle as a specific place, instead of a generic jungle. On Solara, the Jungle that had a particular meaning due to the presence of the Hellcats.

After moments of sputtering some angry sounding syllables, Lordano begrudgingly began stripping off his fine clothing. With a scornful look towards Mackey and Wilson that promised this wasn't over, he hostilely said "Vaffanculo," stepped through the doorway and closed the door behind himself.

Stooping to collect the clothing and shove it unceremoniously into a bag, Wilson spoke to Mackey over their commlink. "Yet another satisfied customer," shaking his head slightly. "What did he just say?" he asked.

Glancing over to Wilson, Mackey snorted. "My exosuit translated it from some long dead and forgotten language as 'leave in a reproductive manner.' The translation package for that language was loaded from the databanks we got from Terra Station."

Wilson shook his head. "Hard to believe we lost our own planet's history due to The Fall, but rediscovered a lot of it on a colony that itself had forgotten about. Really makes you wonder what else we're going to find out in the dark."

Looking towards the doorway Lordano walked through the doorway, Mackey changed the subject. "That was, what, the fifth murderous look we've received? The first one or two promised an interesting day, but by now they're just disappointing. It's like getting asked to dance over and over, but the band never starts playing music."

Tossing the bag into the back of a truck, Wilson agreed with Mackey. "Yeah. Don't threaten us with the same good time if you aren't gonna follow through. Who's next for processing?"

Mackey was momentarily distracted by Lordano's loud, still angry, appearance at the far end of the processing station. He was haranguing the Marines posted there about the unacceptability of the plain clothing they had issued to him. Looking back at Wilson, he answered his question as the Marines scanned Lordano, looking for hidden weapons and other contraband.

"Faction Ullr. Echo 6 and 8 are accompanying them," Mackey said.

Wilson was surprised. "ACCOMPANYING them? Well, at least their processing might be different. Scuttlebutt says they got into a scrap with some overgrown kittens."

Mackey gave a hand signal to the Marines who were escorting Lordano towards the Bulldog parked at a makeshift landing zone a short distance away. They waved back in acknowledgment and ushered Lordano towards the Bulldog that would transport him to Cerberus. Then he looked back at Wilson.

"Their report said the kitties are some sort of lethal, genetically modified Bengal tiger from Earth. They're twice as big and strong, have claws stronger than the hardest steel, and have primitive linguistic capabilities. They're called Hellcats, and are quite smart," Mackey noted.

Wilson was impressed. "Genetically modified? Sounds like more ancient technology that we lost due to The Fall. Why would they have modified those things to be even more lethal and then bring them to this planet?"

Mackey shrugged. "The Ullr say it was because of some sort of apex predator that had been on Solara when humans colonized it. A killer lizard or something. The Hellcats were created and brought in to hunt them to extinction because they had been so troublesome. Eventually, the Hellcats replaced the lizards out in the wild, but they tend to keep to themselves, with one exception. When Ullr Faction youths go into the wilds on a Sojourney, they're supposed to kill a Hellcat and bring back its razor sharp teeth as a rite of passage into adulthood."

Perplexed, Wilson turned to look directly at Mackey. "And if they fail?"

"Then the Hellcat ends the youth," Mackey said simply.

In the distance, the Bulldog's engines began spinning up in preparation for liftoff. Dust motes began swirling with the rising power of the Bulldog's engines.

"Geez. I've heard of some strange coming-of-age rites, but that one is pretty crazy. Wouldn't they run out of Hellcats with all those Sojourners?" Wilson asked.

They both watched the Bulldog quickly rise into the air and vanish from sight before continuing.

Mackey shook his head. "I guess not. I asked the same question. Something to do with the Hellcat's birth rates. Part of their modifications included a much higher birth rate. Used to be the two groups tended to keep each other balanced and somewhat stable in terms of numbers, although lately the Ullr slowly are expanding their population. Eventually the imbalance in that math will put an end to the practice."

Wilson pulled up the Arrivals list inside his visor and checked it to see who was next to arrive. "Speaking of Ullrians, they're incoming to this position. ETA 10 minutes."

The next 10 minutes passed swiftly, neither of them saying much. Their exosuit audio inputs clearly transmitting the sound of jet engines approaching. There were multiple planes in the air.

Mackey turned towards the rising sound, and increased the magnification on his visor. He could see a formation of five military aircraft. A small transport, escorted by five Tomcats from Cerberus was slowing and dropping in altitude to land in the clearing the Marines had designated to receive the incoming aircraft.

Once it landed, Mackey and Wilson, without saying a word, walked towards the transport. As they approached, the exit hatch began to open and the steps from the hatch extended to the planet's surface.

Both Mackey and Wilson stopped in surprise when Echo 8, Lance Cpl. Hiro Gozen, stepped through the hatch first. His black exosuit had four long scratches gouged into the extremely tough, inky black suit material. Hellcat teeth hung on a strap that he wore around his neck, and several non-regulation decorations and Ullrian weapons were attached to his exosuit. Gozen quickly scanned for threats before motioning for someone behind him to exit. His body language was quite aggressive.

An Ullrian woman appeared from the hatch, dressed in the common manner of Ullrian women with leather skins for pants and a leather jacket. For a human from a heavy-gravity world like Solara, she was tall, with pale skin, raven black hair and warm, very dark brown eyes with the beginnings of wrinkles at the corners. The woman gracefully followed Gozen down the steps. Echo 6, Pvt. Julio Gonzales emerged next from the hatch. Echo 6's exosuit bore scratches similar to Gozen's. Mackey could swear it was some sort of strange battle damage that looked just like claw marks at this distance. Echo 6's body language matched that of Echo 8's, and he, too, wore teeth around his neck. The two Marines were obviously quite protective escorts.

Another thing Mackey and Wilson couldn't help but notice was that the Ullrian woman was beautiful. Not just pretty, but stunning. Powerfully built, as was common in the heavy gravity, Delegate Frida Enginnsdottir bore several visible battle scars as would befit an Ullrian shield maiden. As the Ullrian transport lifted off and returned the way it had come, the small party approached the decontamination tent. No words were exchanged between Mackey and Enginnsdottir's newly arrived Marine escorts because they already knew what to do. They had confirmed receipt of the LT's orders prior to their arrival.

The next Bulldog arrived, its engines whining as it set down and waited to ferry Enginnsdottir to Cerberus after she was processed by the Marines. As Mackey watched while it landed, Wilson broke into Mackey's thoughts on a private commlink. "Think we ought to give the LT a heads-up about Echo 6 and 8? The way their exosuits are adorned with new weapons and emblems, they look like Ullrian Marines now."

Glancing over at Wilson and shook his head. "Negative." he said simply. "Echo 6 and 8 have already briefed the LT about their appearance. LT is factoring their somewhat Ullrian appearance into the security plan aboard Cerberus. The Captain agreed Echo 6 and 8 should not appear to be impartial security to give the other delegates a visual reminder that the Confederacy is a zealous friend, and a terrifying enemy. The rest of the Marines will continue to appear impartial at first, but be very protective of the remaining delegates at the same time."

The processing of Delegate Enginnsdottir concluded swiftly. Wearing the nondescript clothing provided by the Marines, she walked up the ramp of the Bulldog waiting to transport her to Cerberus along with Echo 6 and 8.

The engines of the Bulldog began revving up as the pilot prepared for takeoff. The Bulldog quickly rose and vanished into the air while Mackey and Wilson watched from the ground.

"We're going to be busy for a while," muttered Mackey over the commlink.

Wilson nodded his head now. "Yeah. Political intrigue. Ancient blood feuds. Big egos. Mmmmm. Can't wait." Wilson's tone said he'd rather do anything but deal with all that.

The next delegate would be arriving for processing soon.

CHAPTER 37

CERBERUS

"Captain, I'm a fabricator, not a fashion designer," grumbled Lt. Kristoff Alphonso, head of the ship's Fabrication department. Alphonso didn't mention he also majored in college in Computer Design, Mechanical Engineering and Robotics. "I'm the last person who should be deciding what stylish apparel is."

Commander Mueller snorted and traded a glance with Captain Ronin. They were seated in Alphonso's "office," which was really just a small corner of the compartment occupied by Fabrication. She leaned forward with raised eyebrows while responding. "Well, THAT's a relief. I'd hate for the crew to be walking around in lab smocks all day."

Alphonso's eyes rolled at Mueller's humorous snarkiness. So did Ronin's.

"Can you do it or not?" Ronin asked.

Sighing, Alphonso nodded. "Yes. I think. Maybe? I'll need some expert assistance."

"Expert?" Ronin sounded confused. The frivolous world of high fashion was foreign to him.

"Yessir. Expert. Our computers can easily give us the design specifications, so it's an issue of locating suitable designs. The delegates don't want to dress like shapeless blobs, and our regulations prohibit non-crew from dressing in our uniforms for security reasons. We don't know what to do."

Ronin and Mueller sat back in their seats, and Ronin slowly exhaled and nearly whistled in the process. "So, you're saying we need to find a fashion guru aboard a spaceship during an interstellar exploration mission, choosing among a crew that has been far away from civilians for most of the past several years?" Ronin said, glancing over to Mueller with a perplexed look.

Mueller immediately exclaimed, "Don't look at me! I've been here the whole time, too. I wouldn't know what's fashionable if it ran me over."

Alphonso and Ronin laughed.

"Oh no, no! I wasn't thinking of making you suffer like that," Ronin said. "I just pictured having to tell the Admiral that our interstellar space exploration mission failed because we didn't think to have fashion designers aboard."

Ronin was referring to their commanding officer, Adm. Jessup Rodding, who was stationed aboard Wayside Station. Rodding was a product of West Virginia, and his meetings with Ronin and Mueller were often an occasion for Rodding to serve his favorite, dark caramel-colored bourbon, "Old Prohibition."

That mental image caused Mueller to laugh softly. "Admiral Rodding? Can you imagine telling Colonel Hobson that?" Mueller was referring to the ever-mysterious Colonel Hobson of Fleet intelligence.

Neither Ronin nor Mueller were too sure whether Hobson was his first name or his last name. Or, for that matter, whether that was a real name at all. The enigma that is Hobson spoke with an upper-crust British accent, and appeared to be of Indian descent, although no one seemed to know for certain.

Now it was Ronin's turn to imagine trying to inform Hobson, with his dark eyes, intense gaze and no-nonsense manner.

"Yeah. Telling Hobson we needed fashion designers is something that just doesn't compute for me," Ronin said softly. Both Alphonso and Mueller smiled and nodded. It didn't for them, either.

The three were startled when the ship's AI spoke. It had never occurred to the three of them to ask the AI about fashion knowledge.

"Captain. There is one crew member who minored in fashion in college. That person is Junior Protocol Officer Leroy Greene, who was dubbed 'Mr. Deuce' by Lance Cpl. Hiro Gozen and Pvt. Julio Gonzales during their flight to the surface in the escape pod."

Alphonso looked very confused. "Mr. Deuce? What kind of moniker is that?"

"The nickname was bestowed because ..." the AI started to respond when Commander Mueller interrupted.

"That's sufficient, AI. We don't need that particular data," she said, trading amused glances with Ronin.

"Lieutenant, connect with Greene and leverage his expertise in fashion design and social protocols to come up with suitable clothing for our guests. AI, advise Greene of his new orders to assist Lieutenant Alphonso. The rest of the delegates won't arrive for several hours yet, so you'll need to hurry to make this happen," Ronin said, standing up as he did so. "Lieutenant, keep us updated as to your progress and if you need anything."

"Yessir. Expect to hear from me soon," Alphonso said as the meeting broke up.

Ronin and Mueller walked out of the compartment into the corridor beyond. "Lieutenant Gustav says he and the AI have compiled quite the list of possible security threats to our delegates," Ronin noted as they walked towards the Bridge.

Mueller nodded. "I saw the list. There are the usual types of assassination attempts like shooting, stabbing, blunt force trauma, ambush, etc. How are we going to defend against the more creative ways to off a target, like multiple-stage poisoning?"

They stopped at a hatchway as Ronin looked right at Mueller. "They devised a plan for us to keep the delegates separated, while giving the appearance of not deliberately keeping them separated. It's pretty elaborate, but most of it will occur out of sight at the same time."

Mueller laughed softly. "I saw the manpower assignments! We've got an all hands on deck approach ..." she began saying when Ronin's commlink chimed with an incoming message. Mueller fell silent so Ronin could open the commlink.

"Gustav to Captain Ronin. The Ullrian Delegate just arrived with Echo 6 and 8. Sir ... I think Delegate Enginnsdottir's Marine escorts took your orders to appear biased and protective of her more literally than we anticipated." Ronin's eyebrows shot up at Gustav's vocalized concern. Mueller cocked an eyebrow in confusion.

"How's that, Lieutenant?" Ronin asked.

Gustav didn't hesitate. "Sir, I think you might want eyes on this. I'm in the hangar bay."

Trading glances, Ronin and Mueller shared a look of concern. "On our way, Lieutenant. We'll be there momentarily."

***

Ronin and Mueller were able to arrive quickly at the hangar bay, as they had been nearby when Gustav commlinked.

They entered the hangar bay from the large hatchway leading to front of the ship. Delegate Enginnsdottir was still present along with Gonzales and Gozen. The three of them were standing in front of Gamma 4, Pvt. Victor Berger, and from a distance Ronin and Mueller could see some sort of confrontation was playing out, with the Marine escorts standing in front of Enginnsdottir to prevent Berger from reaching her. Gustav had been waiting for Ronin and Mueller near the front entrance.

Without waiting to be asked, Gustav reported to Ronin and Mueller. He spoke softly to avoid being overheard, and wasn't wearing an exosuit like Gonzales, Gozen and Berger. "Captain, Commander. I was about to step in and order Echo 6 and 8 to allow Berger to scan and search Enginnsdottir, same as we did all the other delegates who arrived."

Ronin deliberately assumed a neutral expression as he watched his two Marines. They suddenly nodded towards Berger and stepped aside to allow him to in-process Enginnsdottir. They put on a show of being quite protective of their delegate, and their displeasure at Berger's role was plain to see. But it wasn't their attitude that prompted Gustav to call Ronin and Mueller. It was how they were dressed.

"They look like the Ullrian version of a Marine," Ronin noted.

"Yessir. And it gave me a new idea," Gustav stated.

Mueller and Ronin looked back at Gustav. "What are you thinking?" Mueller asked.

"Sirs, I'm now thinking the other Marines assigned to escort delegates should go ahead and adopt similarly styled looks for their exosuits that are suitably representative of each Faction. It takes our previously decided theme of showing the delegates we are the greatest of friends and the worst of enemies to a new level," Gustav said.

Nodding thoughtfully, Ronin agreed. "Alright. If, and that's a big if, a delegate doesn't object to the practice, make it happen but within some field expediency parameters. And it also helps differentiate which Marine is protecting a particular delegate for Cerberus crew who aren't plugged into Tacnet in case there's trouble."

"Very good, sir." Gustav saluted and, throwing a look at his three Marines standing with Delegate Enginnsdottir to confirm there wasn't any more commotion, stalked off to his office to follow through with the new orders and provide some clarity around them. Mueller and Ronin watched him go, then Mueller turned to Ronin.

"Captain, I'm not too sure about allowing modifications to the uniforms. They could become too ... colorful. That could cause confusion at the wrong moment," Mueller said, visibly concerned.

Ronin shook his head slightly. "Normally, I would agree with you. But the Marines have a long history of making adjustments and adapting to new environments. Lieutenant Gustav was telling me about that history a few months back. He knows field expediency parameters in this context means crafting some strict guidelines for Marine escorts during the Congress."

Mueller's expression changed to one of surprise. "That's what you meant by that phrase? I wouldn't have been able to guess without the rest of the context. You know Gustav can also be rather creative, right?"

Ronin laughed. "Know it? I'm counting on it!"

Mueller laughed as well. "The Congress kicks off in 18 hours. I have a feeling these delegates are in for a few surprises."

Ronin nodded.

CHAPTER 38

CONTINENTAL CONGRESS

Wearing his standard gray fleet uniform, Captain Ronin walked into the main conference room on Cerberus. Escorting Ronin were Marine Pvt. Ty Jeffries, and Cujo. Lieutenant Gustav had insisted that Ronin have a security escort at all times. It was both for his protection, and for the Captain to be seen as intimidating to the delegates.

Ronin wished there was a larger and more regal chamber to hold the proceedings. Unless he was willing to repurpose a hangar or landing bay on the flight deck, the main conference room would have to do. Seeing as Cerberus was in high orbit around a relatively hostile planet and there was plenty of flight traffic beyond the exclusionary zone around the ship that was actively being enforced, Ronin was definitely not going to shut down his flight deck.

Conversation inside the main conference immediately died upon Ronin's entrance. Ronin's gray eyes scanned the room as he stepped to the small podium that had been placed on the table. The large room was fairly crowded with seven Faction delegates seated around the table, seven Marine escorts in exosuits standing behind them, Dr. Wright, and now Ronin, Jefferies and Cujo. The first thing Ronin noticed was that none of the delegates were looking at Ronin. Instead, they were staring at Cujo with varying degrees of curiosity and fear.

Another planet where dogs didn't exist, Ronin thought to himself with satisfaction as he glanced behind and to his right where Jeffries and his Rottweiler, Cujo, had positioned themselves. Ronin had seen Cujo in action before, and knew the highly trained beast was not one to be trifled with.

Another observation confirmed his previous orders. Delegate Enginnsdottir was seated several yards away from Delegate Lordano. Given their Faction's history, keeping them separated to start the Continental Congress was deemed prudent. Ronin also noticed only the Marine escort assigned to Delegate Enginnsdottir had a Factionalized appearance, so he was interested to see long it would take before the other delegates wanted escorts with some personalization. Ronin decided the time had come to deliver his remarks.

"Thank you all for attending. I am Dan Ronin, Captain of the Confederation warship Cerberus. Centuries ago, Earth and Solara were part of a growing human civilization among the stars. That society was destroyed in The Fall, severing all connections between the two planets.

"Solara's largest cities were destroyed during The Fall by an ancient enemy which has only recently been vanquished. This you all now know. What your history is missing is what happened on Earth.

"The Fall was a cataclysmic war so ruinous that the nuclear and biological impact wiped out the planet's entire civilization. Nearly every city was lost. Our cultures disappeared. Every government ceased to exist. Humanity mostly reverted to barbarism. Pockets of technology and a few human settlements survived, thus saving our species from extinction on its own mother planet. As you can see by the arrival of Cerberus in this system, humanity has made a comeback and now we are in a period rapid expansion and discovery.

"How did Cerberus get to Solara and the Alioth system? While we have discovered what we tentatively believe to have once been one of the ancient jump gates linking our worlds beyond the edge of this system, we do not know how they function. We also believe the jump gate back near the Sol system was destroyed during The Fall.

"Each of you is here to represent both your Faction, and to do something which has been missing on Solara for centuries. You are here to represent your colony at the dawn of a new era where humanity reunites. Solaran historical records say there were three colonies—Solara. Forrestal. And, Celestra. On Earth, those legendary names have become known as the Lost Colonies.

Ronin paused briefly for dramatic effect before continuing. "Solara is the first of the legendary Lost Colonies to be rediscovered. Your Factions have sent you here to set aside Factional politics and explore the possible parameters of Solara's relationship with Earth, and other colony of Terra Station."

After a few more minutes, Ronin concluded his opening remarks. He saw his words had the desired effect reflected in the quizzical looks on the faces of the delegates. *They're wondering what kind of FTL drive Cerberus has, and learning of the existence of another colony named Terra Station is obviously a shock to them*, he thought with satisfaction. *Let's see how learning the ancient legends are true plays out now.*

With a nod towards Dr. Wright, who stood up and walked over to the podium, Ronin bade the delegates the best of luck in their endeavor and exited the main conference room.

CHAPTER 39

WAITING GAME

"Three DAYS?" erupted Commander Mueller. She and Captain Ronin were sitting in his ready room adjacent to the Bridge. "Why would it take three days just to choose just one among the seven of them to serve as the Speaker of the Continental Congress? There's no way they should be moving that slowly!" she fumed in frustration.

Ronin smiled tiredly in response and he held up his hands, palms raised, to placate her. And maybe to protect himself a bit, too. "I know. I know! It's dumbfounding how little progress they've made since they started three days ago until you consider how deep the roots of their mutual animosity goes. Centuries of assassinations, open warfare, cold wars, trade wars, cultural wars. The list goes on and on. Despite all that, at least no one did anything as stupid as researching and creating weaponized viruses, which is what the Asiatic Collective did. We all know that resulted in The Fall."

Mueller's left eyebrow rose as she considered Ronin's comments. "No civilization-ending plague apocalypse ... Well, at least Solara has got that going for them, I guess." She still didn't seem satisfied.

Then they both smiled slightly. The moment was interrupted by Ronin's collar commlink chiming, and he quickly answered it. "Ronin here."

"Captain, this is Lieutenant Gustav."

"Go ahead, Lieutenant."

Gustav sounded slightly alarmed. "Captain, we've got a situation developing with the delegates. Can you come to the main conference room?"

Ronin and Mueller traded concerned glances. "On my way, Lieutenant."

Seconds later, Ronin was joined by Private Jeffries and Cujo as he exited the ready room onto the Bridge. Soon they entered the main conference room to discover a chaotic scene.

"You witch! I swear I will kill you!" Duke Lordano shouted at Delegate Enginnsdottir. Private Addington (Gamma 5), Lordano's assigned Marine escort, forcibly restrained Lordano, who angrily pointed towards Enginnsdottir and struggled to escape Addington's grip so he could get to her. Gamma 5 had positioned himself between Enginnsdottir and Lordano, so Lordano was trying to go through Addington.

Enginnsdottir had remained seated throughout Lordano's outburst, disdain displacing her disciplined poker face so briefly that all who noticed later wondered if they had imagined it.

Standing behind her with his hand gripping the pommel of a Monosabre attached to his exosuit was Lance Corporal Gozen. His body language left little doubt Gozen intended to draw the deadly weapon if Lordano got any closer.

Strident voices from the other delegates blended together in the confusing scene, as most of them were already on their feet. "Get him outta here!" shouted Ronin over the noise, while Lordano continued to resist Addington, whose exosuit powered strength was winning the struggle over the 1.5 G muscles of Lordano.

A loud, angry, deeply bass growl suddenly froze everyone. In response to a command from Jeffries, Cujo had used the commotion to position himself between Lordano and Enginnsdottir, and his bared teeth only emphasized the Rottweiler's muscles and capacity for violent action. Cujo began barking, adding to the ruckus.

Lordano decided to step up his game and take advantage of the distraction. He suddenly pushed off Jeffries to gain some separation, taking the Marine by surprise with the reversal in direction. Lordano then brandished a hidden weapon, a blade the length of a forearm, and leapt towards Enginnsdottir. He never got there.

As if materializing from nowhere, Gozen's slashing Monosabre swatted away Lordano's weapon. At the same time, Cujo bowled Lordano over in a fury of biting, tearing, growling, and claws. Somehow Lordano retained possession of his weapon and attempted to defend himself from Cujo, until Private Jeffries caught Lordano's arm. Lordano made strangled noises that sounded somewhere between a cry of fear and a howl of pain or rage.

While Jeffries and Lordano struggled, Cujo continued his assault. There was a sudden cracking sound, followed by the loudest howl yet from Lordano. Jeffries had broken Lordano's arm off at the elbow. Literally.

By now, more Marines flooded the room. Several grabbed Lordano after Cujo had been told to stop. Lordano was quickly trussed up and hauled away to the ship's brig.

Still holding the forearm, Jeffries walked over to Ronin. "Captain, check this out. Lordano's forearm bone was actually a hidden blade weapon."

Eyebrows rising, Ronin looked closely. Jeffries was right. "Huh. Sharpened bone with skin covering an assassination blade. That's not detectable by a scan. Not ever."

Jeffries nodded. "Yessir. Turning your forearm into a bladed weapon is a total commitment to a cause. That kind of fanaticism will be very difficult to deal with."

"What caused Delegate Lordano to go after Delegate Enginnsdottir like that?" Ronin asked, while watching Enginnsdottir approach them as the other delegates returned to their seats.

Enginnsdottir answered the question before Jeffries could. Shrugging sheepishly, she said, "My apologies, Captain. I did not expect Delegate Lordano to react so poorly to the news of his brother's death."

Confused, Ronin asked, "What does his brother's death have to do with you?"

Looking surprised that Ronin hadn't already deduced the answer, she replied, "I killed him. We raided a small, seaside resort on the Cosa Nostra continent of Italia last year because several Dons of ruling families were there."

Without Ronin saying a word, the slow rise of Ronin's eyebrow prompted Enginnsdottir to add, "Lordano tried to use women and children as shields. He died without honor. Delegate Lordano did not react well to learning it was I who killed his brother."

Enginnsdottir exchanged a lingering look with Ronin for a few moments before breaking her gaze away. With a nod to both Jeffries and Ronin, Enginnsdottir returned to her seat.

After she left, Ronin glanced at Jeffries and quietly noted, "She deliberately timed that revelation to trigger Lordano and take him off the board before he could become the Speaker. She just outplayed both Lordano and the Cosa Nostra Faction in a single move."

Nodding slightly, Jeffries glanced down at Cujo, who was sitting alertly at Jeffries' feet, while keeping watch over the remaining delegates. "Yessir. That she did. Impressive," he said just as softly via his exosuit's external speaker so only Ronin could hear it.

Ronin couldn't help but notice his pulse had quickened during the long look into Enginnsdottir's eyes. *Best you settle down there, champ. She's beautiful AND deadly. And not for you*, Ronin thought to himself.

Ronin walked to the podium. The hubbub in the main conference room died down as the eyes of the remaining delegates and the Marine escorts looked at him expectantly. "Delegates, thank you for giving me your attention. Delegate Lordano's actions were ... ill advised. And his injury was unfortunate, but also quite obviously unavoidable.

"Each of your Factions agreed to certain conditions prior to committing to this Continental Congress. One of those conditions was to set aside personal animosities a delegate may have with another delegate. Another condition was that any Faction caught in an attempt to harm another delegate would forfeit the right to have their voice heard in the Continental Congress. Faction Cosa Nostra has now forfeited its right to participate in charting Solara's path forward and its return to interstellar space for the next few years."

As he said this, the Marine who had been escorting Lordano suddenly lifted the assigned seat for Lordano using one arm, and he walked it out of the main conference room without a word. It was a symbolic action that Ronin had ordered well in advance, because he had figured on a delegate or two misbehaving during the Congress.

Ronin's words sunk in. Each Faction wanted access to deep space, Earth and the colony of Terra Station. The benefits of such access were obvious for trade, exploration, and growth, especially if such access could be under favorable terms. Giving up the chance to influence how that all that is structured, and a several year ban on accessing any of it, would seriously hurt the interests of a Faction.

Ronin continued on. "As was made clear to your leadership, the Confederation is not requiring you to accomplish anything here. Solara is free to do what it will. But ..." and here Ronin paused for dramatic effect, "the Confederacy is also free to do what it chooses as well. And it chooses to offer the benefits of membership, free trade and society to worlds whose individual nation or nations guarantee the rights of all citizens under a peaceful and unified form of government.

"Planets whose individual nations are warring upon one another instead of cooperating to create a functioning, stable society aren't worth the investment of the Confederacy's time and resources. With that, delegates, I will leave you to your work."

Ronin finished, and he left the room with Jeffries and Cujo in tow. The doors to the main conference room closed behind them.

Several steps into the passageway outside stood Dr. Wright, Commander Diane Mueller and her husband, Karl. They both had thoughtful expressions on their faces.

"What?" Ronin asked.

Eyebrow raised imperiously now, Diane said, "Membership? Free trade? I think we have a budding diplomat on our hands here."

Before anyone else could say anything, Karl chimed in. "Mmmmm-hum. Definitely the stuff of a senior statesman. Captain, I think you missed your true calling."

Ronin's eyes rolled slightly and he groaned in exasperation.

Quite entertained, an amused Dr. Wright decided to poke Ronin's bruises a bit, too. "Oh, Captain. Yes, I agree. I would be happy to recommend you to the laureates at the Diplomatic Institute." Wright deliberately said it with a very enthusiastic tone of voice that he knew would push Ronin's buttons.

Ronin didn't quite manage to conceal the look of horror that briefly flashed across his features. "I really hate you guys," he said with a small shake of his head. "I think it's better if I toss you lot out the airlock and continue this mission in peace and quiet."

Wright and the Mueller's tried to maintain their faked earnest-looking expressions, but one glance between them and they burst out laughing at Ronin. He shook his head again as he walked in the direction of the Bridge.

Jeffries threw a quick salute and nod of his head in Diane's direction before following Captain Ronin. Even in his exosuit, Diane had no trouble discerning the fact that Jeffries was hiding a huge grin at their banter behind his visor.

Karl looked at Dr. Wright after they left. "You didn't mean that about the Diplomatic Institute, did you?"

Dr. Wright snorted with a laugh. "Heavens no! Once you two started in, I just couldn't resist tormenting the Captain like that. Everybody knows how much he would despise being a politician. And that man would probably just go and kill politicians who annoy him anyway."

"Hmmm. Sounds like we should definitely make the Captain a politician then," Karl replied.

"Ha!" Diana laughed with a shake of her head. "That's the last thing the Captain would want. He'd rather chew broken glass. Anything but being a politician."

CHAPTER 40

BREAKTHROUGH

"**C**aptain, this is Dr. Wright. Speaker Enginnsdottir would like to visit with you if you have a moment."

Normally, summoning a ship's captain like that wouldn't go over too well, but the past few weeks had proved highly unusual. Ronin had been thrust into a role mixing the duties of a host, guardian, fierce warrior and wise advisor. He had gotten to know each of the remaining six delegates on a personal level, and was now on a first-name basis with all of them.

That was especially so with Frida Enginnsdottir. Since her election as Speaker, she had met with Ronin many times. Blinking sleep away, and rubbing his face in his hands for a moment, Ronin replied, "I'm in my quarters as it's my sleep shift. Where does she want to meet?"

There was a slight delay as Dr. Wright apparently checked with Enginnsdottir. "Captain, if it's alright with you, the Speaker says your quarters are fine. She doesn't want to force you to traipse around the ship in your sleeping clothes."

Wright was trying to be professional, but Ronin thought he nonetheless detected an amused tone in Wright's voice.

"Yeah, that's fine. I'll leave the porch light on for her," Ronin said. He quickly threw on his uniform, brushed his teeth and ran a comb through his hair.

Minutes later, the chime at the entry announced her arrival. "Enter," Ronin said.

The doors automatically opened to admit her into Ronin's quarters. Dr. Wright had already departed, so only Enginnsdottir stood at the entrance. She walked into his quarters, which were quiet as Ronin's two children were asleep in their small rooms.

"Dan, I'm sorry to disturb you like this in the middle of your night," she said.

Ronin grinned. She was both beautiful and a forceful presence. She also was very forthright, which he couldn't help but appreciate.

"Anything, Frida. I did say I'd be available whenever the delegates need me to be. What's on your mind?" he asked as she approached him.

Enginnsdottir touched his arm and looked up into his eyes for a few moments before inhaling, almost as if she had forgotten to breathe for a few moments and suddenly remembered the need for air. She shook off the moment to return to business.

"Um. Oh yeah. Ah, we wanted to flesh out your ideas for future exploration a bit more. Are the crews for the future missions solely composed of naval personnel from Earth, or would they be joint missions?"

Surprised, Ronin thought for a moment. It was a pretty technical point, and not all of those points had been fully discussed. "Well, I should think they would be joint missions in the sense that all the officers and crew would be Confederate Navy personnel, but the navy would draw its personnel from Earth, Solara and Terra Station. As a practical matter, it would be years until the captains of such missions aren't all from Earth because of the time it takes to gain the necessary experience in commanding a ship, but eventually the Captain ranks would include Solarans and the Terrans.

"The Navy is adamant against nepotism, and very egalitarian in that a person's origin should play no role in their advancement through the ranks." Ronin was acutely aware of Enginnsdottir's close proximity while he stammered through his thoughts. He felt like he was babbling just to keep her close.

Nodding, Enginnsdottir looked into his eyes as she agreed. What Ronin was proposing was not only quite fair, but very practical as well.

"You know we must maintain the appearance of neutrality for the crew and the delegates?" Ronin asked, drawing in a small breath. The pounding of his heart was threatening to damage his ribcage at this point.

A small smile formed at the edge of Enginnsdottir's lips. She shook her head slightly, before suddenly reaching up and pulling Ronin's head down towards hers. "Then let's not tell them," she said simply as she kissed him.

Ronin could not resist any longer.

CHAPTER 41

NEW BEGINNINGS

Ronin's commlink chimed. "Ronin here," he said after opening it. "Captain, this is Lieutenant Gustav. The Speaker wishes to speak with you if you have a few minutes free."

After several months aboard Cerberus, the Continental Congress had finally wrapped up and the delegates were preparing to return to Solara. "Tell her I'll meet her in my ready room," Ronin acknowledged.

"Very well, sir. I'll escort her there myself," Gustav said as he ended the commlink.

Ronin guessed that Gustav must have anticipated Ronin's choice of location and had already been leading Enginnsdottir to the ready room, because less than 30 seconds elapsed before he heard the door chime announcing someone was waiting admittance. "Enter," Ronin said.

Enginnsdottir walked in without a sound, and the door closed behind her. She was dressed in a gauzy, flowing white outfit that both hid her form, and highlighted her shape at the same time. Ronin swallowed hard when he saw her.

"Dan," Enginnsdottir said softly after a moment of returning his gaze. "I wanted to say goodbye personally before I return to Solara."

Nodding, Ronin regained his composure. "It was a pleasure to get to know you these past few months. I ..." he began to say before the rest of the words he planned to say just failed him.

Enginnsdottir smiled sweetly as she stepped close to Ronin. Putting her hand on his chest, she looked up into his eyes. "When will I see you again?"

Ronin liked to think he was doing an admirable job of controlling his breathing up until then. He really wasn't that good at it, and while Enginnsdottir certainly noticed, she was similarly unsuccessful. Now that they need not stay apart for the sake of the Congress any longer, their feelings for one another had risen to the surface.

"I have been wondering that same thing for weeks," Ronin said. The life of an unattached ship's captain was, by necessity, a solitary one.

Enginnsdottir was undeterred. While she and Ronin had kept their relationship discrete and away from prying eyes, the two of them had talked a lot about the future. Specifically, their own future and how to have one together.

Taking Ronin's hand into her own, Enginnsdottir slipped off a braided leather bracelet from her hand and she put it on Ronin's wrist. This was clearly a symbolic action by Enginnsdottir, but Ronin wasn't quite sure what it meant.

Sensing Ronin's confusion, Enginnsdottir leaned up and whispered into his ear. "I am no longer Speaker, and am my own woman again. Your people still need you, and you cannot leave them. My people do not need me further and I can pursue my own path. I choose to walk my path with you, Dan Ronin."

She pulled back and looked into Ronin's eyes, her eyebrows arched questioningly.

Ronin had several questions, but this answered the biggest one. The others just didn't matter that much all of a sudden. He smiled softly, their gaze never wavering. "Yes," Ronin said simply, before they kissed.

A few minutes later, Enginnsdottir walked out of the ready room and greeted Lieutenant Gustav, who was still waiting for her. "Thank you for all that you've done the past few months, Lieutenant. Um, I'm ..." she began saying, when Gustav, who wasn't wearing an exosuit, interrupted.

"Not leaving us after all, ma'am?" he asked, with a raised eyebrow and the corner of his mouth upturned into a satisfied smile as he nodded in the direction of Enginnsdottir's quarters.

Startled, Enginnsdottir glanced at Gustav. "Wha ... Were you eavesdropping somehow?" she asked as they walked.

Still wearing a satisfied smile, Gustav shook his head. "Ma'am, I know my Captain. I've seen him at his best, and his worst. He is a fearsome leader, with an unyielding determination in the face of grave danger. I've also seen another side of him from what you see aboard the ship, and that's when he's with the family whom he loves dearly. That other side of him has also appeared with you after the two of you started spending all that time together."

They reached the main conference room as Gustav remarked on the change in Ronin. The room was empty except for Gozen, who turned when they walked in. He had been gathering up the baggage and Enginnsdottir's personal belongings for their return to Solara. Gozen glanced at the two of them, both of whom had a surprised, "hope no one heard that" expression on their faces.

Breaking into a huge, knowing smile, Gozen simply asked, "Shall I leave these right here then, ma'am?" Like Gustav, he wasn't wearing his exosuit, either.

"You, too?" Enginnsdottir asked, surprised.

"Oh, yes ma'am. While the delegates where closely escorted and kept segregated from one another outside Congress, the Marine escorts saw and heard everything," Gozen replied as he set down the luggage just as Commander Mueller also walked in.

Mueller didn't miss a thing. "Geez. It's about time the two of you figured out your situations. You're staying with us, then?" She asked in a hopeful tone. Mueller sure didn't want Ronin to resign, and felt certain he would not ever consider such a thing while the ship was in deep space.

Enginnsdottir just nodded. She was still trying to process how it was the crew seemed completely aware of her and the captain's relationship.

Smiling broadly, Mueller looked at Gustav and she stuck her hand out while motioning for Gustav to pay up. Shaking his head slightly, Gustav made a small show of grudgingly reaching into his pocket and placing it into Muller's hand.

"You win, ma'am. Fair and square," Gustav said.

"Win? Win what?" Enginnsdottir asked.

Mueller happily answered the question. "We had a small wager on when the two of you would come to your senses. Lieutenant Gustav was a big romantic and figured it would be just as you would have boarded a shuttle to return to the surface. I thought you weren't into making a big, dramatic scene like that instead of quietly deciding to stay on."

Mueller's explanation made everyone to laugh. It seemed as if the entire crew knew what had been going on.

CHAPTER 42

UNION

Admiral Rodding glared at Ronin, the menacing squint in his eyes providing a stark contrast to the soft Wisconsin sunshine. Ronin tried to withstand the power of Rodding's gaze, but he fidgeted uncomfortably as he stood in his dress blue uniform. A trickle of nervous sweat suddenly ran down his side, adding to Ronin's growing discomfort in the cool, springtime air.

A small zapping sound caught Ronin's ears, which also brought to him the distant crashing of the spy drone that was just burnt out of the sky by a Naval security crew who was determined to keep pesky news cameras from invading the private event.

When Rodding shifted his powerful glare to Frida Enginnsdottir, who was standing next to Ronin, his demeanor suddenly softened and he exchanged smiles with her. He could see she was clearly as nervous as Ronin.

A few giggles escaped from Sarah and Edward Ronin, who stood behind the couple and were enjoying the unusual sight of their famous father struggling with his nerves.

Rodding leaned slightly to get a clear look at Sarah and Edward and gave the two a knowing wink before he began to speak. "Then, by the powers invested in me by the Confederate Navy ..." Rodding said, pausing with a nod towards the huge Ullrian warlord standing next to him. The heavily armed man's powerful muscles caused the leather and furs he wore to creak slightly, as they stretched and strained across his expansive frame.

"... and blessed by the holy warriors of Ullr ..." said the warlord solemnly, dipping his head forward slightly as he said the ritualistic words.

"We now pronounce you husband and wife," Rodding finished, breaking into a broad grin.

As Ronin and Enginnsdottir kissed, there was a raucous roar of cheers and clapping behind them because the crew and Marines of Cerberus had elected to attend. It didn't hurt their mood that Lieutenant Sunderland had brewed a special beer for the occasion, or that Captain Ronin and Admiral Rodding had opened the bar for them two hours ago.

Minutes later, the newlywed couple found themselves approaching two lines of fierce warriors facing each other and standing at attention. On the left were Confederate Marines, wearing their dress blues with ceremonial swords at their sides. On the right were similarly armed Ullrian warriors, wearing their usual leathers and furs. A shouted command from Lieutenant Gustav startled Ronin. The two lines of former enemies drew their swords as one and formed a saber arch. It did not escape Ronin or Enginnsdottir's attention that it was actually an arch formed from Solaran Monosabres wielded by both lines of warriors.

The couple glanced at one another and shared a grin before striding forward under the arch into their new lives together.

CHAPTER 43

EPILOGUE

"So, where are you two honeymooning?" Rodding asked before sipping the dark caramel-colored Old Prohibition. Ronin had made sure plenty of the Admiral's favorite bourbon was stocked for the reception. The party around them was in full swing.

Ronin took a sip of champagne and they both gazed at the cold waters of Green Bay from the viewing balcony of the reception hall for a moment. The setting of the springtime sun and the water's reflection of the sun's last rays made the view even more beautiful. The Wisconsin-made bubbly was from the nearby Door County peninsula. It was Ronin's favorite champagne.

"We're going to spend a few quiet days at the family cottage in the Northwoods to start with, then Frida insisted we tour some of the larger cities and excavations around the planet. I had wanted to spend all our time at the cottage and away from any media attention, but she was horrified at the thought of visiting Earth and not seeing any of the attractions," Ronin said, before taking another sip.

Rodding snorted and sipped the bourbon again, this time taking more time to savor its rich flavor. "Ah. Good call on stocking my favorite stuff, Dan. And I should imagine Frida was very convincing about wanting to see the home planet."

"You try saying no to a Shieldmaiden from a 1.5G planet and see how that goes for you, sir! The excavations of the ancient pyramids on the African continent and those structures they've begun exploring in southeastern Europe seem to have captivated her imagination. She's fascinated by all the lost civilizations that once existed on Earth and discovering that many old legends were actually true."

Rodding nodded thoughtfully. "The historical records from before The Fall that you brought back from Terra Station have begun filling in many gaps here on Earth. Those pyramids are from a long lost nation that was once known as Egypt. The other is a structure called the Acropolis that was located in another bygone nation known as Greece. Both existed so long ago that the archaic records of a long lost civilization which you brought home themselves refer to the even older lost civilizations as ancient by comparison."

Now it was Ronin's turn to nod his head as he took in this information. It was hard to wrap his head around the idea some deceased civilizations existed so long ago that antiquated records from a dead civilization described those even older civilizations as ancient.

Their conversation was interrupted by the approach of the Ullrian warlord Jørgen Freyr who had helped officiate the wedding ceremony. Freyr carried fresh drinks for Rodding and Ronin, and handed them to the two men with a nod. His voice carried an accent that he didn't bother to conceal now, as he had done for the ceremony.

"You talk of ancient civilizations, yes?" Freyr asked, taking a sip of bourbon before looking at his glass of Old Prohibition appreciatively with raised eyebrows.

Rodding, being a bourbon aficionado, noticed Freyr's appreciative expression. "My favorite," he said with a nod towards Freyr's glass. Freyr acknowledged Rodding's statement by clinking glasses with him before taking another sip.

Freyr reached into his tunic, withdrew a crystal data chip and handed it to Rodding.

"What's this, Jørgen?" Rodding asked as he took the chip.

"Now that my people have joined the Confederacy, we wish to contribute immediately. The Confederation has legends about Earth's former colonies, and now the legend about Solara has come to life. My people think another old legend may be true as well," Freyr said mysteriously. His pause to take another sip of bourbon only added to the dramatic flair imparted by his words.

"We believe that chip contains the location of *Forrestal* and instructions on opening a jump gate," Freyr stated.

Rodding and Ronin traded stunned looks.

"THE *Forrestal*? The Lost Colony?" Ronin asked in disbelief. His wedding reception just took a totally unexpected turn.

To be continued...

FORRESTAL

Book #4 in the Cerberus Series

After rediscovering the Lost Colony of Solara and surviving the conflict between the Factions of Solara, the newlywed Captain Ronin and his crew are sent back to deep space to look for the Lost Colony of Forrestal. The crew of Cerberus never expected to use a working jump gate, find a colony with a malignant culture, and battle advanced technology from before The Fall.

The story continues in the next installment of the Cerberus series.

About the Author

This is author John Filcher's third book in the Cerberus series. A former Green Bay resident, he is getting acclimated to life in Minnesota.